zero tolerance

Zero Tolerance

A Murder Mystery

Byron "Putt" Riddle

Byron "Putt" Riddle

iUniverse, Inc.
New York Lincoln Shanghai

Zero Tolerance

A Murder Mystery

iUniverse books may be ordered through booksellers or by contacting:

iUniverse
2021 Pine Lake Road, Suite 100
Lincoln, NE 68512
www.iuniverse.com
1-800-Authors (1-800-288-4677)

This is a work of fiction. All of the characters, names, incidents, organizations, and dialogue in this novel are either the products of the author's imagination or are used fictitiously.

ISBN: 978-0-595-42386-6 (pbk)
ISBN: 978-0-595-86722-6 (ebk)

Printed in the United States of America

Writing and getting a book published for the first time has been a humbling, but gratifying experience. It wouldn't have happened without a lot of people pitching in one way or another to move my writing "Zero Tolerance" along. Many of them offered their encouragement to me. Others brought their skills or expertise to the table to help me. Their help ranged from advising me about their field of work or participation to commenting on the way I wrote certain passages that they thought needed to be clarified or changed. It included of course some correcting my spelling, grammar and punctuation. For all these people I appreciate your taking the time to help me.

And hoping that I leave nobody's name out that played a role in one way or another, here is a list of them. I start with my family, my wife Virginia and my four children, Michelle, Brent, Kyle and Katie Beth. Then I want to say thanks to Tom Hawkins, Mike Mitchell, Addis Charless, Mal and Jeanette Whitsett, Pat and Karen Sasser, Gwyn Eakins, Brenda Hendrix, Rex and Dana Doss, Doug and Marlene Rand, Richey Cutrer, Dennis Wilson, Cody Wilson, Sue Lown, Karon Golden, Tibby Niehues, Lynne Grimes, Dawn James, Jodi Wright, Kali Birkes, Carolyn McGilvray, Don and Linda Hansen, Laura Oswalt, Gean Craig, Kenda Eckols and of course the "Pie On The Porch" gang, Stan and Linda Mitchell, Virginia Bounds, Sheila Higgins, Elaine Bounds and the best pie baker in the dental profession, Dr. John Sponenberg

CHAPTER 1

Kim Whittaker and Leslie Reeves were on their third time around the concourse on the home side of Barrett Bradwell Bumblebee Stadium just three hours before the kickoff of the big non-district game between their hometown Honey Oaks Bumblebees and another perennial powerhouse of Texas 4A football, the Turnersborough Tornadoes who were coming in from over 200 miles away out in west Texas. It was to be the fifth meeting in the last three years between the strong rivals. A pattern had been set between Honey Oaks High and Turnersborough High in the previous two seasons. The third game of the year in mid September, they faced each other in a non-district game. Then again in November of the Texas 4A UIL playoffs, the Bumblebees and the Tornadoes had met in the third round going on to the state quarter-finals. In the past two years, the winner in September had been the loser in November. Honey Oaks had moved on to the next level two years earlier. Last year had been Turnersborough's turn to advance. With all the state polls paying attention to both schools' stellar records of the last two years, the teams were ranked in the top 10 4A schools in Texas football from the preseason on through the first two games that each team had played to open the new year. Blowout wins in those first two games over hapless opponents had the Bumblebees and the Tornadoes riding the polls as the fifth and sixth best 4A teams in Texas respectively. Prognosticators writing in the big city papers in Dallas, Houston, and Austin had this Friday night meeting of the 4A powers as the game of the week in all Texas classifications. For that reason and the results of the previous four meetings between the two teams, the fifth game was a sellout of all 10,000 seats at Barrett Bradwell. There even promised to be a large crowd of fans who weren't able to get the coveted tickets to this most anticipated game who would show up hoping for a miracle that would somehow get them inside the gates of the regal structure that rose prominently into the sky, its red brick walls covered in ivy on the outside.

It was the promise of big profits coming to the Honey Oaks Booster Club from that sellout crowd that had Kim and Leslie making their way around the concourse once more on the home side of the 50 year old stadium. For they were near the top of the echelon of parents that made the Booster Club the most highly successful volunteer organization in Honey Oaks. As they walked, the two moms of Honey Oaks High students kept up an animated line of chatter about their responsibilities and duties in making sure that the Booster Club's role in the game proved to be an unqualified financial success. Both of them were clad in the broad banded shirts in alternating colors of black and yellow that faintly resembled the thorax of a bumblebee. They also both had on the same type of black pants which showed off their cute figures to the utmost. On their feet were the yellow tennis shoes that matched in hue the yellow color that had been picked along with the inky black color and the team name "Bumblebees" back in 1918 by a student body anxious to recover from World War I and to start the football traditions that would make Honey Oaks High a special place for generations of students in the west central Texas town. The Booster Club had special ordered 300 pairs of shoes in that yellow color from the Nike Shoe Company. As with every other product that the Club sold to raise money to finance its aid to Honey Oaks High athletics, the shoes had been an instant hit and quickly sold out. Kim, Leslie, and 298 other parents, grandparents, ex-students, and fans had bought the shoes at a marked up price that put an extra $7500.00 into the Booster Club coffers.

Kim, a perfectly-proportioned brunette some five-foot-six-inches in height had her shoulder length dark hair streaked in that same yellow color, an effect that caused the men she was passing by on the stadium sidewalk to turn around and look longingly at her as she walked away from them. Leslie, right beside her, bounced as she walked, a five foot-nine inch package of vitality and friendliness. The constant smile under her blond curls with which she greeted everyone approaching her confirmed that warmth. But what really made the two women stand out as special to the people was not their physical attractiveness, but instead was a combination of their standing in the Booster Club and who their children were. Which of those factors weighed the most in determining how Kim and

Leslie were regarded by the citizens of Honey Oaks couldn't exactly be determined.

Kim held the position of Club Treasurer. As such, she had been very pro-active in building the Booster Club's assets with one fund raiser after another which had the Honey Oaks High fans decked out in the distinctive black and yellow colors of their beloved Bumblebee teams. Besides the aforementioned tee shirts, pants, and tennis shoes,that merchandise included sweatshirts, caps, and blankets. If they weren't wearing the merchandise, they were otherwise buying the individual game ribbons, supporter signs, Bumblebee noise makers and the Stinger Stickers for their yards. The Bumblebee noise makers were devices mounted on handles which Honey Oaks fans would hold and rotate in a spinning manner. The effect was that when everyone on the home side of the field were doing this together, the air flowing through the slots in the devices made it sound as if it were a swarm of bumblebees attacking anyone getting close to their hive. The Stinger Stickers were meant to be displayed in the front yards of Bumblebee fans. They consisted of a black and gold colored conical device which tapered down into the shape of a stinger. Inside it was a 30 inch metal spike, a foot of which extended beyond the stinger and ended in a sharpened point to enable a Bumblebee fan to easily put it in the ground in his or her yard.

The other claim to fame for Kim besides being Booster Club Treasurer was that she was the mother of William Thadeus Whittaker, the senior quarterback of the Bumblebees. Tad as he was called by everyone who had known him since he was born was a six foot-three inch, 215-pound talented, smart athlete who was in his third season as the starting signal-caller for the Bumblebees. A great passing arm coupled with just enough speed and agility to avoid sackers and his football smarts had earned Tad not only All-District honors, but also All-State recognition. He made the third team 4A Texas roster his sophomore season. Then despite the Bumblebees losing out to Turnersborough High last season in the playoffs, Tad's offensive output numbers had jumped so much that the sportswriters around the state had voted him a notch higher at second team All-State for his junior year. As a result of the past two year's performances and the first two games of this season, Tad had been named to the top state and national recruiting prospect lists. The Whittaker mailbox usually had letters everyday from colleges all over the country as well as from avid alumnae of those schools urging Tad to make their individual school the place to further his education.

And perhaps just take that chosen institution of higher learning to a national championship or two along the way.

Likewise, Leslie had gained renown as a tireless worker at the Booster Club annual Bumblebee Golf and Tennis Extravaganza. She also set out at each home game the aptly named "Honey Pots", metal depositories anchored to the railing at three different spots along the concourse on the the home side of Barrett Bradwell. Fans were encouraged to throw their spare change if not a dollar bill or two into the Honey Pots with the proceeds going to help buy all the Bumblebee athletic teams in every sport extra workout equipment or facilities to give Honey Oaks High that extra edge in athletic competition. But more importantly to the fans, Leslie was the organizer and coordinator of the Honeybees. The Honeybees were 16 girls from the high school, eight juniors and eight seniors who made up the extra spirit squad besides the regular cheerleaders. It was with their enthusiastic dance routines that the Honeybees raised the spirits of the Honey Oaks fans. But the fact that they were all beautiful girls very physically fit also contributed to their aura. Leslie oversaw a workout regimen that not only made them tops in performing their dance steps, but also maximized the display of their young curves in the form-fitting costumes of black and yellow stripes. The bottoms of their leotards had little fanny packs sewn into the rears and shaped to look somewhat like cute little stingers which they vigorously shook during some of their dances much to the delight of the crowds watching them.

Leslie had gotten the Honeybees started two years earlier when her daughter, Tara Ann said that she was through with the dance classes that she had started a dozen years earlier as a four year-old kindergardener. Tara was ready for new challenges and desparate to get out of the weekly lessons that now seemed so little-girlish. She had grown into a younger version of Leslie and was drawing a lot of attention from the boys at Honey Oaks High. She relished that attention. It was an easy sell for Leslie to get her interested in being a part of the Honeybees and continue her dancing in this group that would easily be the center of attention at school functions. The success of the Honeybees left both mother and daughter very satisfied with their roles in being a part of it.

Kim said, "This is going to be a great day. The Booster Club ought to pull in the dough."

"Yeah", Leslie responded, "I've even got my cousins in Dallas who have bought tickets to the game asking if they can spend the night after the game is over. I told them come on and bring their bedrolls. We would just make it a big slumber party afterwards."

"Are those the ones who graduated from here in '85?", queried Kim. "I thought that they hardly cared about the Bumblebees anymore."

Leslie answered, "With the way the Bumblebees have played the last two years and gotten so much attention statewide, it's become a source of pride to say that they graduated from Honey Oaks High. Tad has really helped build that reputation the way he's played."

As they reached the middle of the concourse with the 50 yard line just below them, Kim tossed her head in pleased agreement, "I am so proud of Tad, but always worry he's going to get hurt badly in a game. But right now I'm worried about Justin. We haven't seen him yet. He said he would get here right after the market closed. That was over an hour ago. He was going to bring our money to make change in the Bumblebee Hive when people coming to the game want to buy stuff."

Leslie replied, "He probably had a client not happy with the way the market did today that he had to deal with. As I was driving in, I heard them say on WBAP that the Dow was down 45 and the NASDAQ 82. He'll be along any minute."

"I sure hope so.", said Kim. "We have everything ready to go and our club volunteers working this game all said they would be here by 5:30. So, we just need Justin to have stopped by the bank and gotten our change from the tellers. Of course he has the key to open the Bumblebee Hive up too." The Bumblebee Hive was one of those conical shaped buildings that had been installed just beyond the entrance and served as the shop from which the Honey Oaks Booster Club sold its merchandise, tickets to fund-raising activities and dinners, and held its weekly meetings during the school year. It had been painted to look like a big bee hive looming over the football field.

Leslie came back, "Hey, not to worry if he's running late. I have my extra key to the Hive with me. I had to go by this morning and drop off some CD's for the Honeybees to get after the game. It has the music for our new routines at next week's game. And the Band Boosters running the concession stand said that we could borrow a few hundred from them to run the Hive if our money was not here on time."

"Just the same," Kim said, "I'm still a little worried that Justin's not here yet on the biggest game of the year." She reached into her pocket and pulled out her cell phone. As she flipped open its top, she said, "I think I'll try him and see where he is." She punched in his number and put the cell to her ear. After a half minute of waiting, she heard his message, "This is Justin Slater at Thompson Brothers Investments. I'm not available right now, but please leave your name and number and a brief message and I'll get back to you as soon as possible. If you need immediate service to place an order or ask about your account, please call the toll-free number shown on the bottom right-hand side of your statement. Thank you for calling. Have a good day." Kim snapped the cell shut in frustration and shoved it back into her pocket. By now, they had moved past the tiers of seats at the end of the stadium closest to the entrance gates. The Hive was 200 feet away.

"C'mon Kim", Leslie ventured as she reached inside her tummy pack safely secured under her Bumblebee thorax shirt and pulled out the spare key to the Hive. "It' s still 30 minutes 'til our workers get here, but we can open it up and make sure it's ready to go. I thought it looked okay when I was there this morning."

Somewhat reassured,Kim said, "You're right Leslie. We do have a good Plan B in place and we can start to do it until Justin gets here." They reached the Hive and Kim stepped back to let Leslie unlock the door. No sooner did Leslie open the door and step inside than she backed right out nearly tripping over Kim who was right behind her.Kim saw that her face was drained of its color and her mouth was wide open in horror though no sound came out of it. She stepped into the Hive around Leslie to see what had brought on this reaction from her.

What she saw made Kim back out of the door just as fast, but her mouth was not frozen silent. She was screaming loudly, "Oh my God! Oh my God! Somebody help us!" Her cries began to draw the few people who had come early to Barrett Bradwell to the Hive to see what was happening.

A peek inside the door of the Hive showed that Justin Slater was there. The Justin Slater who had followed in the footsteps of his father and gone to work for Thompson Brothers Investments in Honey Oaks after college. Under the tutelege of his father, Barton Slater, Justin had become a very successful stock and commodity broker. When Barton Slater had retired 10 years ago, Justin was picked by the regional vice-president of Thompson Brothers to succeed his father as the Honey Oaks branch manager. For the most part, Justin had prospered in that role certainly making the money, but also making some enemies along the way from unhappy clients to brokers he had terminated over the years to an ex-wife who had pitched a heated divorce fight with him. Generally though, life had been good for the native Honey Oaks High and Aggie graduate. He was well regarded enough around town that he had been elected to three terms as president of the Honey Oaks Booster Club. That exposure had been good for his brokerage business. In turn, his love for his town and his high school had made his service to both of them highly appreciated. But now that service and dedication were over. There wouldn't be a chance for a fourth straight term as the Booster Club president for Justin. For what Leslie and Kim had seen was his lifeless body laying in the middle of the floor face up in the Bee Hive. There were blood stains all around his chest covering the floor. Above his torso, a Stinger Sticker rose in the air, its bottom plastic part resting on his black and yellow, now crimson-colored Bumblebee shirt. The 12 inches of metal spike used to anchor the Sticker in the ground instead was buried all the way into his chest.

CHAPTER II

The head coach and athletic director of the Honey Oaks High Bumblebees, Matt Donaldson was clearly agitated. It was 8:30 a.m. Monday morning, nearly three days since Justin Slater had been found murdered at the stadium. School, such as it was, had begun on time 30 minutes earlier. But no one, students, teachers, cafeteria workers, administrators and custodians had their hearts in following a regular routine. Nothing had been regular since Slater's body was discovered two hours before the scheduled kickoff of the biggest regular season game for the Bumblebees. Donaldson's agitation came from the way that everything had evolved from that point of discovery up til the current moment. But most of all, his agitation was directed toward the man who had taken over the stadium to begin investigating Slater's murder. That man, Feaster County sheriff, Dalton Gumby was sitting on the other side of Donaldson's desk steadily ignoring all the glares being thrown his way by coach Donaldson.

"Dad gum it Dalton!", Donaldson hissed at his visitor for what seemed like the fifth time in the last 20 minutes, "You've got everything balled up with your crime scene investigation." The six-foot-four-inch 225-pound former tight end, now 40, but still very fit raised up from his chair, placed his hands in the middle of his desk and leaned down menacingly at the sheriff, also a 40-year old, but a mere five-foot-nine inch 170 pounder. Gumby though returned his glare without flinching. "The last three days have been a nightmare for Honey Oaks High! And it's mainly because of the way you've handled Slater's slaying. First of all, declaring all of Barrett Bradwell a crime scene and barring everyone from being there just two hours before we were to play Turnersborough was a disaster. Telling us that we couldn't play our game there since you hadn't made your investigation yet took some balls!"

Gumby softly replied, "But you still managed to get your game in."

Donaldson exploded, "Just barely! We had to find somewhere else to hold it. And we had to deal with all the people from Turnersborough and around the state who came for the game only to be told it was off for then. Boy, talk about a pissed group. The Tornadoes had just arrived on their buses and had to be dealt with. The first thing I did was grab their coach, Robert Thomas to figure out what to do. Someway we had to play the game."

"So it happened Saturday afternoon in Waco.",countered Gumby. "What was wrong with that?"

"What was wrong with that?", replied Donaldson, his voice rising and his face once again getting flushed with anger. "I'll tell you what's wrong with that! First we had to deal with 10,000 fans that showed up an hour after you declared the whole stadium a crime scene. You had the whole complex wrapped with that crime scene tape going all the way around the stadium and not allowing anyone to go past the tape. Talk about a mess! Getting them to believe that there was no game was almost undoable. And then Coach Thomas and I were brainstorming where to go for the game."

Sheriff Gumby moved his chair forward and looked intently, almost ferociously into Coach Donaldson's face. "Matt!",he snapped, "You and Coach Thomas only had to brainstorm where to play a football game. I'm trying to brainstorm who killed Justin Slater and why. The stadium is where it happened. I had to preserve the integrity of this crime scene to have any hope of picking up any evidence from it. So keeping people out until our investigators have finished there is all that I could do!"

Donaldson came right back at him, "Sheriff, Coach Thomas and I nearly came to blows over the way you shut down the stadium. I was mad over losing our home field advantage when we were the game of the week in Texas high school football. He was mad because he first thought what you did was a stunt to psyche out his team. And they had been on the road three and a half hours just getting here."

Matt Donaldson brushed his hair back and put his Bumblebees cap back on his head. When he calmed down, he resumed talking, "Thomas finally asked me, 'What do we do? Where do we go?' "I replied," There's only two stadiums not too far from here that are big enough for our crowd and also available for us to use, Amon Carter Field at TCU and the Waco ISD Athletic Complex. The Waco Complex turned out to be the best deal financially for both schools so we went there. But we lost the game because we were so unsettled having to move it from here."

Gumby looked momentarily perplexed at that revelation from Donaldson. Then he spoke again, "You'll get over that loss, maybe even play better the rest of the season because of it. Slater's not ever going to get over what happened to him. Frankly though, I'm under a lot of pressure from a lot of people on this one. I even brought in the Rangers Special Crimes Unit to help me. We have nothing so far, but we'll be through here maybe early this afternoon. Then you can get Barrett Bradwell back to use again."

Hearing that made Donaldson relax somewhat. "Thank God! We need our field to get ready for San Montevido coming here Friday. And maybe that will pacify the Honey Oaks Booster Club. Kim Whittaker has been all over my case that the Booster Club has been ruined financially for the year by not being able to sell their stuff on Friday. The Waco ISD athletic director would have let them sell our school stuff at their Complex. But it was of course all stored in the Bumble-bee Hive where Justin's body was. You wouldn't even let them take anything out of it to take to Waco to sell since that was the center of the crime scene."

He continued, "Mrs Whittaker also let me know as Tad's mother that she thought his scholarship chances got hurt by the way the game went in Waco. Three interceptions, no touchdowns and only 133 yards for him. Talk about a mad mama!" Then he added, "But that's not all. Our school district along with Turnersborough lost over $8,000.00 in ticket revenue that we had to pay to play over there. The Band Booster Club lost out on all its concession sales. A crowd that large would have easily spent $7,000.00 here. The Chamber of Commerce has called on behalf of a lot of its members who didn't get to cash in as planned when the game got moved. About the only ones who made out were the gas stations and convenience stores when most of the Turnersborough fans at least filled up when they decided to head home and wait until Coach Thomas and I figured out where to play the game. Heck Sheriff, I've even had the staff at the Ingleside Retirement Home all over me since this happened. Their residents like to come over here and get in their daily walks on our track. It gives them a sense of security to be in the enclosed area out of the traffic. Locked out, they had to do just like the Bumblebees and go to Murphy Park for their workouts. They can't wait for this to end."

"Actually neither can I Matt", responded Gumby as he rose from his chair and headed for the door. "We will let you know as quickly as we can when you can have your stadium back. Hopefully in a few hours," With a nod of his head toward Donaldson, he was through the door and gone, closing it softly behind him.

CHAPTER III

As Sheriff Gumby was leaving Coach Donaldson's office with both men still obviously frustrated over the conversation they had just had which was more confrontational and unresolving than either of them wanted, in another part of Honey Oaks, the world was more peaceful and settled at least for one of its visitors. That part of Honey Oaks was Murphy Park, a 64 acre oasis of beauty and function which lay just inside the city limits on the eastern side of town. Inside the park, the landscape was hillier and the land more undulating than most of the land around it in Feaster County. Underneath its earth was an outcropping of limestone which went deep enough to make that area untillable compared to the other rich soil of the land next to it. What did grow there in abundance were stands of oak trees. Scattered sporadically among the oaks were some cedar trees that had come up unobtrusively where birds flying overhead had deposited their droppings from above. Around and underneath the trees were various grasses, Side Oats Grama, Little Blue Stem, Blue Grama, and Big Blue Stem.

A spread of Texas wild flowers with their array of vivid colors completed the scenic beauty of Murphy Park. During a year visitors there were treated to the sight of blanket flowers, blue bonnets, Mexican hat, Blackeyed Susan, Golden Spread columbine, cone flower and Indian paintbrush. The flowers also attracted bees seeking nectar. The stands of oak trees had become home for their bee hives. Hives hung from the branches of the oaks or were found in the cavities of dead or dying trees.

That was what the early settlers of Feaster County discovered as they moved into the area around 1850. They established a trading post just west of the Murphy Park area because of the creek and springs bringing water down from the higher elevation of the outcropping. With the rich soil and pleasant climate which allowed for long growing seasons, the settlers bought the land around there to begin their farming. From that initial trading post, a whole community developed. Mercantile stores, banks, churches, stables, cotton gins, homes, and schools were gradually built in this part of Feaster County. Those early settlers noted the presence of the oak trees, their bee hives, and honey combs dripping with honey and naturally named the community springing up just west of it Honey Oaks.

The land for Murphy Park was a tithe from Jeremiah Murphy in 1925 to the city of Honey Oaks. He owned a section of land which with the exception of the acreage where Murphy Park would be was filled with the rich soil that made the cotton crops which he raised year after year big money makers. It was after a particularly great year of high cotton prices and big profits that Murphy decided to give the land which yielded nothing to him to the city. That it coincidentally was 64 acres in size or a tenth of a section made it seem like he was tithing. He assigned this tract the same value as the rest of his acreage from which he made his living in taking a deduction on his income taxes that year.

While Murphy Park was hilly and undulating in most parts, it did have a broad low lying area big enough in size to be used for team sports. The City of Honey Oaks took advantage of that and began building fields there starting about 1955. It hauled in enough dirt to even out the slope for a softball diamond and a baseball diamond. Then came two football fields for youth football teams to play their league games. As soccer became popular in Texas in the 1970's, Honey Oaks managed to fill in enough additional area for four soccer fields to be built. Enough parking space was added for a lot in the middle of the athletic-recreational complexes and along the roadway going through it so that families could get close enough to unload their lawn chairs and place them along the sidelines of whichever field was being used by their children or spouses for a game.

It was in the middle of the soccer fields that Tad Whittaker and two other senior Bumblebee players were doing impromptu passing drills with a bag of footballs they had brought from Honey Oaks High. The other two seniors, Larry Collins and Desmond Washington were both wide receivers and had caught a lot of balls thrown by Tad starting back in fifth grade together. It was okay for the trio not to be at school even as Sheriff Gumby was pulling away from the campus in his patrol cruiser some 45 minutes after classes had begun. Through extra study times and dual credit courses they had been taking the last two years, the senior trio had whittled down the number of courses at school that they still needed to take to graduate to four apiece. Since Honey Oaks High operated a seven classroom periods daily schedule, the last period was for athletics which blended into after school practices for the various team sports of swimming, football, volleyball, soccer, fall tennis and cross country played by Bumblebee athletes. The threesome was not required to be at school until third period began.

Tad, Larry and Desmond were working on passing routes that the Bumblebees would be using against San Montevido Friday night at Barrett Bradwell. The throws from Tad to Larry and Desmond were even more on the money and crisper than what he had been doing in the season to date, especially the disastrous Turnersborough game in Waco last Saturday. Larry and Desmond, both rangy six plus footers were running short routes and long routes. Tad was delivering the ball to them at just the right moment on each throw. When either one ran a route which called for him to make a sharp veer to the sidelines at the last second, he would turn and find a pass on its way to his outside shoulder, placed where a defender couldn't get to it. The ball could easily be cradled in his arms once he made the cut.

Tad was throwing at his best because he was feeling at his best for the first time in the last three months, since the day he had made a devastating discovery in his own home in early July. The one he had been unable to talk to anyone about even though he was so bothered by it. In reality, he had been bothered for the 18 months before that by his parents' marital problems. There had been a lot of arguments between his mother Kim and his father Robert which ended with slammed doors as one or the other left the room or house to cool off. The fights were often followed by periods of a truce or at least no fighting though the atmosphere was filled with tension between his mom and dad. Those periods were as combustible as dry grass in a six month drought. The wrong word spoken, a shrug of the shoulder taken the wrong way and other slights, either perceived or real was enough to escalate his parents back into a full-fledged fight Finally after one really bad argument, Tad's dad Robert had packed up and moved out to an apartment a few blocks away. His mother had gone ahead and filed for divorce eight months earlier in December. However, it was still pending.

After that the battling had almost ceased completely, but Tad was heartsick over Kim and Robert and him not being together as a family. When he could, Tad urged them separately and together to put their marriage back together. The division of his family was the only thing marring what otherwise had been a near-perfect life for him. But neither of his parents seemed inclined to patch things up. They were content to be in their own separate spaces. They both told him how much they loved him anyway. In his school activities, they even came together peacefully like attending the Bumblebee Booster Club meetings and working on committees that had special projects going to help Honey Oaks High. But when the meeting or activity or project was over, they went their separate ways much to Tad's sorrow and chagrin. Still for some reason the divorce had been put on hold. The fact it had not been finalized gave Tad hope that his mother and father would get back together soon.

That hope got shattered totally the first week in July. Tad was working part-time for the Crawford Brothers Feed and Seed Store in a summer job. He got to work both indoors and outdoors in a variety of tasks for the store. One of those tasks involved moving pallets of feed, seed and fertilizer into stacks as high as six pallets in the air. He had just finished helping a customer load her purchases into her pickup when Jerry Crawford, one of the owners called out to him, "Hey Tad, we need a pallet of that number 3 fertilizer up front since everyone is clammering to put it on their yard before the rains hit this weekend. Go get the lift and bring it to the front." Tad started in the direction of the forklift. Then Crawford stopped him, "Whoa! Where's your safety helmet?"

"I left it at home this morning, but it's just one pallet. I won't need it."

"Tad you know the rules. Our insurance company coverage requires all employees to wear them when doing jobs like that. Not to mention the government inspectors who can drop by anytime unannounced. That could cost us big bucks. And we're not even talking about what could happen to the Bumblebees and your scholarship chances if you got hurt here. Run home and get that helmet!"

Tad jumped into his pickup and drove to his house getting there a little after noon. His mom, Kim was supposed to be away from the house all day seeing his Aunt Kathy, her sister in Dallas. So he didn't figure on having her fix him a sandwich while he was there on this quick trip home. Instead he would just grab his helmet and go through the drive through lane at Texas Burger on his way back to

Crawford Brothers. Inside his house which he had entered quietly, he was making his way to the hall leading to his room when he heard sounds coming from his parents' bedroom. Puzzled by it since no one was supposed to be home, Tad walked toward that bedroom which was down a short hall leading from the family room and on the other side of the house from the wing which contained his bedroom and a guest bedroom connected by a bathroom in between them.

The door into his parents' room was partially closed, but open just enough that he could see inside most of the room from a reflection in the mirror that hung on a wall over a chest of drawers opposite the door. What he saw amazed him and sickened him simultaneously. It was his mom and the Bumblebee Booster Club president Justin Slater standing very close to each other in the middle of the room. Neither one of them had on a stitch of clothing. Tad was looking at Slater's front side and his mother's back side from the view that he had. Justins's hands were cupped around Kim's breasts. His thumbs were randomly roaming over her nipples, an action that was drawing soft moans of ecstacy from her. Tad's attention was drawn to his mom's right hand. In it, she held the very erect penis of Slater which she was slowly stroking from moment to moment. Her left hand was on his right cheek caressing it tenderly. They were kissing each other full on the mouth with both of them darting their tongues inside the mouth of the other for the extra stimulation. Tad stood there transfixed, unseen by them, but not believing what he was seeing. He could hear Justin breathlessly intoning to Kim, "Come on. I want to go inside you." With those words, she began to back toward to the king-sized bed just behind her. If Slater hadn't been a willing participant, he would still have gone to the bed with her. For Kim was tugging gently on his stiff member to guide him over there. But he went easily enjoying what her hand was doing to him. She felt the bed at her backside and tumbled backwards onto it pulling Justin down on top of her.

That was all that Tad wanted to see. He made his way to his room, his eyes brimming with tears and retrieved his helmet. Then he quietly left the house making no noise. There was no stopping at Texas Burger because he no longer had an appetite. What he saw had sickened him so much. He now knew that there would be no reconciliation of his parents. And for that, his hatred of Justin Slater was instantaneous and unending. It didn't matter that Slater was divorced and considered very desirable by most of the single women around his mother's age His wealth and his positions both as the top stock and commodity broker in Honey Oaks and the president of the Honey Oaks High Booster Club put him in the spotlight. Tad couldn't even see that Kim might have been ready for a new relationship considering how long she and Robert had been apart and that the divorce was filed and just waiting to be finalized.

Instead he focused on how much he now could blame Justin Slater for the final breakup of his parents' marriage. From that moment on he had nothing to do around Slater if he could help it. He even skipped out on being one of the Bumblebee team members that helped out at the annual Bumblebee Golf and Tennis Extravaganza, the big fund raiser held in early August to raise funds for scholarships for graduating Bumblebee athletes. Before he had been an enthusiastic helper acting as a ball boy at the tennis nets or driving a golf cart loaded with cold drinks for the Bumblebee supporters out on the course. He even missed the Bumblebee hamburger feed that preceded the first morning of two a days when the UIL finally allowed teams to begin getting ready for the season. He said his stomach wasn't quite right and he needed to have it ready for the regimen that Coach Donaldson and his staff of assistant coaches would be putting the Bumblebees through. But the only real reason for his holding back was so that he didn't have to look Justin Slater in the face.

The news that his body had been found inside the Bee Hive made Tad feel like a big burden had been taken from his back. At first, it had been a problem for him and his teammates to have to deal with it and go elsewhere to play this key game. The turn of events put them out of synch more than it did Turnersborough who was planning to play on the road anyway. The Tornadoes were better able to adjust to the Waco ISD Athletic Complex and had demolished the Bumblebees very handily. Tad was going through a lot of emotions from Slater's body being found. Mostly though, it was a relief to him that this perceived adversary was gone never to interfere with his parents again. At long last he felt good about his world, his football and his future without a Justin Slater in it.

CHAPTER IV

After a brief stop at the Honey Oaks Gas 'N Go to get his regular order of a sausage biscuit with cheese and a bottle of Yahoo Chocolate Drink, Gumby continued driving toward the the Feaster County Law Enforcement Center on Bonham Avenue, a block past the courthouse. The weekend had been one of strain and stress for him, perhaps more so than any other situation he could recall in his 18 years in law enforcement. The nasty exchange that he and Matt Donaldson had just had was just a small sample of the outrage and fear being vocalized to him and his deputies over the gruesome murder of Slater and his department's handling of the investigation which not only had inconvenienced a lot of Honey Oaks residents, but also to date had not provided any leads as to who the killer might be.

Now he was hurrying back to his office to be there in time to meet briefly with his deputies for updates on everything crime-related and emergency-related that had taken place in Feaster County over this past weekend. He would give them instructions for their duties for the day, the main focus being to develop leads in Slater's slaying. Then he spent 30 minutes returning calls to concerned citizens and the media, always the media pressing for information to pass on to their readers, listeners, and viewers about his department's progress on the Slater killing. It had gripped the attention of almost everyone in Honey Oaks not to mention Feaster County and the rest of the state. Each media caller explained that he or she had a deadline to meet, whether it was for a noon broadcast or a weekly paper going to press the next day. Each wanted to have the latest to pass on to his or her audience so as to seem to be on top of the story. For Dalton Gumby to have to say, "We have nothing to give you now. Our investigation is continuing as fast as possible." refuted the old saying of "No news is good news." to the reporters anxious to update their audiences.

Those tasks out of the way, Dalton leaned back in his chair and slowly ate his cheese sausage biscuit in between swigs from the bottle of his Yahoo drink which had gotten warmer sitting on his desk while he talked to his deputies and returned his calls. Still it tasted just fine considering how little he had gotten to eat since the 911 call came from the stadium Friday afternoon. Leaning back in his chair was also a moment of luxury considering how much he had had to maintain an upright posture in dealing with all the people that were either a part of or were trying to project themselves into the unfolding drama. It was at a moment like this that he wished Betty Ann was there to give his shoulders and neck a quick massage and temporarily take the tension away.

But Betty Ann was long gone from his life, a victim of breast cancer some three years earlier. She and Dalton had been together for 15 years when the deadly disease had taken her, despite double mastectomies and radiation treatments that had prolonged her life for four years after the initial diagnosis. It was ironic that Betty Ann had been a registered nurse working in the intensive care ward at Honey Oaks General Hospital many times taking care of patients who had just gone through cancer surgeries. To them Betty Ann dispensed her own specialty of TLC to ease their pains and discomforts. That was what Dalton had received from her when his job had him under stress. It used to make the difference for him, but he realized that it would never be again. He just had to get back to solving Justin Slater's murder.

He called out to the front office to his secretary, Linda Owens on the inter-office line, "Linda, did you get hold of Clayfour Peterson for me?"
"Yes I did Dalton. He said that he would be here about 10:30."
"Good", replied Gumby. "Just send him on in when he gets here." With that he closed his eyes and leaned back in his chair once more. Knowing that Clayfour would soon be there made him relax for the first time since Slater's body was discovered. He started drifting off.

"Sleeping on the job again! You must have figured out who killed Justin and are just waiting for the right time to pop the story." Gumby came to just in time to see the grinning face of Clayfour Peterson staring down at him, his cold blue eyes twinkling as he stood just inside the office door jamb. Peterson good-naturedly winked at Gumby his "just kidding" signal. A 50-year-old, he carried 230 pounds on a six-foot-two-inch frame that had a little bit of a gut pooching out above his belt. His thick brown hair had started showing flecks of gray through it two years earlier. He came on into the office and slid down into one of the two blue leather wing back chairs there for visitors and employees seeing Gumby.

Dalton said, "Clayfour, I'm so glad you're here. I really need your help more than anything else in figuring out who did in Justin" That Gumby could say that to a man who had once been his biggest political rival for the job of sheriff indicated how much each man had retreated from the stances that once had them marked as bitter rivals. Peterson ran twice to take Gumby's job after his first term. He had made charges that Gumby wasn't effective in performing his duties. He focused on a string of thefts throughout Feaster County that were related to the ever escalating energy prices. The price jumps had otherwise honest, but now desperate citizens considering other alternatives to actually paying more dollars for their energy needs. Gumby's chief deputy had caught a break each time and discovered who was doing most of the thieving. The sheriff staged a big raid on their ranches leading a big group of his deputies, three DPS troopers and the Honey Oaks Police Department Theft Division on the raids eight and 15 miles out of Honey Oaks. He had been savvy enough to have the editor of the Honey Oaks Daily Dispatch, Jeremiah Carter along with television reporters and cameramen out of Waco and Dallas there for the raids and subsequent arrests. Gumby ballyhooed their coverage of him at work enforcing the law into sweeping defeats of Peterson in both elections. Moreover it caused Peterson to accept Gumby as an adequate law enforcement officer whom he no longer wanted to strip of his badge.

Peterson even having an interest in a law enforcement career was always a question mark of the Feaster County voters considering his family background and businesses. It had started back in 1892 when his great-grandfather, Harold Clayton Peterson I had built a cotton gin. It was successful from the beginning, ginning more bales of cotton than any of its Feaster County competitor gins. To meet the ever-increasing demand for services from the area farmers, the gin had been expanded in size five times during the last century. To the farmers, the Peterson name stood for integrity, competence and fair-dealing. Not always the case with the owners of the other gins in Feaster and the other nearby counties.

Clayfour's dad, H.C. Peterson III, had further added to the family business empire in 1960 when he invested the extraordinary profits that resulted from the high cotton prices of that year into a new venture for the family. Weather conditions which had hurt the cotton crops on the South Plains around Lubbock never came that far east to Feaster County and its environs that year. Instead the ideal growing conditions made for bumper crops which aided the Peterson family in their own farming operations and in ginning cotton for everyone else, a true financial bonanza. The Peterson Gin and Mill Company had its best year ever. H.C. had looked at what some of the consequences had been for the workers in Feaster County in the leaner years of lower cotton prices. Then bouts of alcoholism, family violence and minor felony crimes took place when the money got tight. Some of those workers faced arrests and jail time when this went on. H.C. decided to establish a bail bond business with some of that cash bonanza. With a base of potential bail customers most of whom that he knew to not be high-risk criminals, but local people temporarily down on their luck, setting up Peterson Bail Bonds was a natural. H. C. could handle their need to be released from jail showing them genuine empathy and discreetness. But crime being a growth industry, Peterson Bail Bonds flourished with the Midas touch and entrepreneurship of H.C.

H.C. assumed that Clayfour would follow right along in the family businesses and take them over at some time. While Clayfour intended to do that, the investment in the bail bond business turned him to a new direction of work that he wanted to follow-law enforcement. Dealing with the few serious criminals who occasionly were clients wheted his appetite to get into dealing with them as a police officer. He had gone off to Tarleton Stat to pursue an agri-business degree just like H. C. had encouraged him to do.In his junior year, a poster was placed on the jobs available board in the student union for classes forming at the City of Dallas Police Academy for new policemen with the promise of a job placement with the Dallas Police Department at the end of successful completion of the four month training course. The next class would begin in January, 1965 right after the fall semester at Tarleton concluded. That was all the motivation Clayfour needed. He applied for the Academy and was accepted. He dropped out of Tarleton much to the chagrin of H.C. to start his new life. After completion of the course, he became a Dallas city cop for the next 10 years. When H. C. suffered a stroke, Clayfour finally returned home to Honey Oaks to take over running the businesses and farming operations. But the law enforcement itch had not been completely scratched until his two failed attempts at unseating Dalton happened.

From then on, he was content to be in the Feaster County Sheriff's Reserve helping out when a real emergency created the need for the reserves to report for duty.

Being the third and fourth generations of males bearing the same name as the patriarch of the family had both its good and bad moments. While the latest two generations of Peterson men outwardly resisted and protested being Harold Clayton Peterson the third and the fourth, inwardly they were proud of the continuation of the same name generation after generation. But to publicly put some distance between their personal pride and the public face they showed to the world, each put a twist on how they were known to their friends, family, business associates and others in Honey Oaks and around. His father simply started referring to himself as "H.C." and printed his cards, letterheads and business signs that way to build his identity. The third was dropped save for the most legal of all business needs.

It had been a lot easier for his son. Harold Clayton Peterson IV started being called Clayfour by his best friend in the seventh grade, Justin Slater.Slater told him then, "My dad thinks your name is too much a burden to refer to you as the fourth. I just like calling you Clay, but I know your dad wants people to know you're the fourth. So I'm going to start calling you Clayfour. It ought to make everyone happy." Slater had nailed it perfectly. From their clique of six inseparable friends to the other seventh graders at Honey Oaks Junior High, Clayfour became his name. It spread to the other grades, the teachers, the parents of the others in Clayfour's clique and on and on 'til finally there was hardly anyone who could ever recall Harold Clayton Peterson IV being called anything but Clayfour.

CHAPTER V

Dalton eyed Clayfour with wonder as to how he could display any kind of humor and light-heartedness at a moment like this. His life-long friend Justin had just been so viciously murdered. He had to be feeling badly for Slater's family as well as for himself given their close friendship which began in the first grade. The 44 years that had elapsed since then had done nothing to diminish that closeness. Clayfour had even been asked by Justin's children to be a pallbearer at the funeral service scheduled for tomorrow afternoon at two o'clock at the First United Methodist Church of Honey Oaks. It finally came to Dalton that Clayfour was burying his sorrow with his attempt at humor. But underneath losing Justin hurt him as much as it did almost anyone else in Honey Oaks.

"Clayfour, I think maybe you can help me figure out who offed Justin better than my deputies and the Honey Oaks Police Department. Certainly more so maybe than the DPS special crimes unit out of Waco."

"That's some pretty good officers you just mentioned. I guess I'm flattered. But why me?"

"Because of your long term friendship with Justin, you've known him and his family, friends and business associates from way back when." Dalton paused, drew in his breath, then continued, "Besides that connection, there are two other things that make you stand out as the one who can help me best. First, you both moved in financial circles not open to everyone in the county. I know Justin was your broker as well. You spent a lot of time on almost a daily basis at Thompson Brothers presumably managing your family businesses and your own personal investments. And there are others like you who're there in that office day by day watching the market, fairly active in it. Sweaters, I think is what they call all of you."

"But Dalton", Clayfour protested, "I may be there most of the time, but mainly I was in Justin's private office either trying to hedge our cotton business or lock in the best interest rates on a short term basis for our bail bond business. Hedging the cotton means taking one side of a futures trade as a farmer and the other side as a gin operator. I have to keep the bail bond money liquid and secure while maximizing the returns on it. There hasn't been much time that I've socialized with the sweaters out in the bull pen."

The bull pen was the large open area where the clients of Thompson Brothers could sit and watch the stock and commodity trades go across on long electronic boards. There were lots of chairs for them as well as a table and bookshelf off to the side that held copies of research services such as Value Line and Standard and Poor's plus the weekly and daily publications like the Wall Street Journal, Barron's and Investors Business Daily. Interspersed among them were research pieces and advisories authored by Thompson Brothers stock, bond and commodity research departments in the home office in Atlanta. Four of the newer brokers who had not yet built their books of accounts enough to a level of production that merited them having a private office were out in the bull pen, their desks inside low wall cubicles that presumably gave their clients coming in for advice and transactions some degree of privacy. In reality though, everything was pretty open and everyone's business became known sooner or later. It got talked about among the sweaters whether good or bad. That was the socializing Clayfour spoke of.

"Nevertheless Clayfour, you're around that office and well-known to where people would talk to you there. Frankly there are people there or who used to be there who could have had it in for Justin."

"You still don't have any solid leads?"

"Not really, that Stinger Sticker had been handled by so many members and customers at the Bee Hive that we couldn't lift any meaningful prints off of it."

"You know, much as I hate to say it, Justin had made some enemies along the way. Anybody calling in any names to follow up?"

"Just a few and they aren't proving to be of any consequence. Good alibis easily proven and that kind of crap so far. But Clayfour, in addition to you being able to hang around Thompson Brothers since you already fit in there, you still have your investigatory skills since being on the Dallas force all those years. I know you can still put them to work and feel you would like to. Lordy, those two races you ran that nearly put me out of this job showed how good you are. So on an unofficial basis, I'd like you to help me out to solve Justin's murder. Him being such a close friend all these years, I know you would like to see justice for Justin."

Clayfour looked at Dalton thoughtfully," Dalton, you've hit the nail on the head. Justice for Justin. I do want to see that most of all. And I do fit in at Thompson Brothers where I might learn something. As I mentioned, there are and were some people there who would just as soon see him dead. Still, he probably had enemies in his Booster Club duties. You know how it is with parents and coaches. If I focus downtown, that ought to free you up to focus on Honey Oaks High. Count me in."

"Great!", exclaimed Dalton. "I was hoping to have you aboard. You can start gathering information and passing it to me asap."

"Okay, but clear up for me one possible motive that I've wondered about since last Friday."

"What's that?"

"Could this have been a robbery that just went bad? It was known by a lot of people that Justin always left the market right after it closed on home game days to run to the bank and pick up the cash to run the Bee Hive. The Turnersborough game was a sellout which meant that the club would probably need more cash on hand than usual. Did somebody knowing his game day routine come to the Bee Hive early to rob him?"

Dalton quickly answered, "No! All the money, $3000.00, was in two bank bags laying by his body. One of the bags was soaked in his blood and it left the cash and coins in a big sticky mess. But we checked with the bank on Saturday morning. Its vice president and cashier Tommy Logan opened up just to let us check this out. All the money the bank gave Justin on Friday was there."

"Well it was a thought. I'll keep my ears open and my eyes peeled. I may learn something at the funeral tomorrow just by seeing who's there. Being that I am a pallbearer and the service is going to end with everybody there walking past the open casket, I will be able to maybe see some people of interest tied to Thompson Brothers. Heck, for that matter, I may spot some other people that will raise my suspicions. You get a broad mix of people going to funerals for reasons other than just paying their respects. Some show up just for the social side of it. Others have this morbid curiosity that gets them out to services. Somebody may be there to admire his or her handiwork in doing away with Dalton."

CHAPTER VI

At 1:50 p.m., Clayfour and the other five pallbearers walked into the sanctuary of the First United Methodist Church of Honey Oaks from the rear door to the left of the chancel. The front row of the left section of the sanctuary was reserved for them. The first six rows of the middle section were resolved for the Slater family. Other than those seats, every pew on the ground floor was completely filled, about 500 mourners. The 200 individual seats in the balcony were also filled. Some 700 people inside the sanctuary. Fellowship Hall was at the opposite end of the long hall which connected the two colonial style wings of the 40 year old building. It was also filled with 300 more mourners who sat in the chairs that the church staff had set up that morning. They were connected to the service inside the sanctuary by the sound system that could be used for any of the rooms in the church to be joined to any other room. Other mourners were lined up in the hallway outside the doors leading into the sanctuary where they would stand throughout the service.

Peterson looked resplendent in his Armani navy blue suit. His white silk dress shirt was offset by a white-dotted dark blue silk tie. It was tied into a perfect Windsor knot. His brown hair was combed straight back, but was short enough on the sides that it made an overall favorable look, especially to the women in the sanctuary who admired his looks and his money and his social standing, but not his married status. Completing his wardrobe were his laced black leather shoes, highly polished and gleaming even in the muted light of the sanctuary. Clayfour looked at his fellow pallbearers and marveled at the diverse group that had been assembled for Slater's last appearance in public. He represented Justin's group of boyhood friends who had remained close to each other in the town they had grown up in. To his right was Phillip Mitchell, the assistant office manager of Thompson Brothers. Long time client Robert Holliday sat next to Mitchell. Sitting to his left from the Slater family came two nephews, Jerry and Barry Martin, the twin sons of Justin's sister Abigail Slater Martin. They had flown in from their classes at the Wharton School of Finance in Pennsylvania. Their granddad, Barton wanted them to be in investments also. Early in their lives, he had prepaid their tuition to Wharton so that they could be as well-prepared in the investments business as anyone could. It would definitely open many different doors for them.

On the other side of the Martin brothers was Justin's Honey Oaks High connection, assistant principal Chuck Johnson who also happened to have graduated from Texas A&M. But that happened 10 years later than Slater's final year in the Corp. Clayfour's gaze to his left was brought short by the sounds of six pewfuls of Slater family entering the sanctuary from the door to the right of the chancel. Everyone in the sanctuary rose and stood until the family had filled the six pews reserved for them. Then the funeral director, Herb Harrison motioned to the congregation to take their seats.

Clayfour noticed that Justin's three children, Julie, Charles and Alton came in to the front row along with their spouses and Justin's mother, 75 year-old Geniveve Anderson Slater. Her older sister Nelda Marie Anderson Porter was right beside her in the wheelchair which the attendant from her nursing home in San Antonio had pushed into the sanctuary. Justin's brother Charlie and his wife Donna sat next to Abigail and her husband Paul. The second row was filled with Justin's grandchildren, nephews and nieces. Cousins filled the next three rows. The last row, in a gesture of reconciliation by Justin's family and at the insistence of Julie, Charles and Alton was taken by their mother and Justin's ex-wife, Phyliss, three of her sisters, two of her brothers and two nieces.

After the family was seated, the service began. Music began with the soloist, longtime family friend Gerald Donahue whose baritone rendition of "How Great Thou Art" brought many tears to the mourners. A couple of songs sung by the entire congregation and Reverend Brad Barlow brought the message of Justin's good works and rich life. There was plenty of mention of his children and his daughter Julie's son Dayton and daughter Debbie, Justin's grandchildren and his love and pride for all of them. Reverend Barlow shifted from the focus on Justin and his family into the promise of eternal life that Justin was now enjoying. He told how it would come later to everyone in the sanctuary, in Fellowship Hall and standing out in the hall. It was assured by God that it would be there for all of them.He reassured them that had been the message delivered by Jesus as recorded in the New Testament in all four Gospels. That said, Reverend Barlow delved into the do's and don'ts that everyone there should follow to assure getting to the place in Heaven reserved for them. He didn't dwell too long in getting his entire message to the congregation because Charles was going to follow him with an eulogy to his father which was at a minimum going to be very emotional and possibly very long as Justin's oldest son poured out his heart about his feelings and those of his other family members for his dad. Charles got up and began to speak.

"My father was so special to not just my brother, sister and me, but to so many other of the kids that we were in school with. They thought of him as a second dad. And he watched over them like a mother hen. If he thought that they were getting into trouble, he would step in to stop them from themselves or from others he thought might bring harm to them. And even though we're out of Honey Oaks High by several years, he still felt the same way about the kids going there now. That's why he has been so perfect as the Booster Club president the last three years. His love for all kids continued on right up until he was taken so abruptly from us last Friday. I just know that there was some student at Honey Oaks who he watched out for this year just as he did for all of us a few years back. That was just his nature to be protective and loving toward his kids.And we all were and are his kids." Charles' talk was poignant, moving and stirring. It had the mourners once again dabbing at their eyes with their handkerchiefs and tissues. Some were outright bawling as the 23 year-old son recounted the special memories that everyone in the family had about Justin. Clayfour glanced back to his right and noted that even Phyliss Slater who had waged one of the nastiest divorce battles ever just three years earlier with Justin seemed as distraught today as anyone else in the family.But he could recall the battles and the threats of violence uttered by Phyliss against Justin. Could she have been still angry enough to have killed him?

When Charles stepped down from the pulpit and returned to his seat, Barlow announced that the service was over except for those wanting to pass by the open casket to pay their final respects. He directed them to follow the instructions of the ushers on how to come forward row by row and section by section. They began to file past the open teak wood casket with a blanket of roses covering its lower half. Each one stopped briefly to take one last look and to mouth good by to their old friend, neighbor, business associate or fellow citizen. Occasionally one would reach out a hand to touch his hand as it lay straight by his side. Clayfour took all this in from his vantage point as the mourners were coming up the inside right aisle and turning his direction to walk past the casket. They were exiting down the left inside aisle before they reached him. It gave him a good chance to see each person and how he or she seemed to be reacting to Justin as they came by.

Several of them he noted were known to have had run-ins with Justin at Thompson Brothers. As far as Clayfour knew, they hadn't exactly kissed and made up with Justin. His demise shouldn't have mattered to them. In that group was a trio who he could list as possibilities to have slain Justin. There was Freddy Benjamin a broker he had fired for his dishonesty. Chuck McGuire had gone broke trading commodities. Dick Nichols who Justin had sued for not paying for a stock trade and then got him blackballed with other brokers came by. Clayfour had those three in mind even before they had passed by the casket and turned parade left at the left aisle to go out. It was the fourth one on Clayfour's mind that he realized either wasn't there or chose not to pass by the casket. That one, T.J. Morgan would be the one who Clayfour wanted to check out first, particularly when he thought of the reason that T.J. might have had in going after Justin. And for that matter, him.

CHAPTER VII

Cotton Row was the popular name given to Bowie Avenue over its 120 years as the cotton industry became a vital economic contributor to Feaster County. The richness of the blackland soil to the south of where Honey Oaks began its growth made that area the most ideal location for the first cotton farms. It was about five miles south of Honey Oaks. To the cotton ginners, locating close to the prolific farms was an easy choice. From 1875 until 1892, there were two gins in the area each one about 200 yards apart. A rough road which came out from Honey Oaks to the farms farther south divided the two gins. Initially the road was wide open prairie, but the more the horse and wagon teams made the trips from the gins back into Honey Oaks, the more it became a visible road now upgraded and maintained annually by the Feaster County Road and Bridge Department.

Harold Clayton Peterson I's timing in building his gin on South Bowie Street in 1892 was perfect. He was able to get the railroad which ran west of the area in a north-south direction to build a spur to his facility. It gave him a leg up on the competition and made his gin an immediate success. Soon other businesses related to cotton farming and merchandising began to spring up along the road. Bowie Street had been created when the city fathers of Honey Oaks had laid out an orderly array of streets and blocks around the first structures in the town. The streets had been named first for Texas heroes. That included those who had died at the Alamo and Goliad to those who had perservered in the victory at the Battle of San Jacinto. After that group came streets named for Southern Civil War leaders and belatedly, the American presidents. All that group of streets were laid out to run north and south. The cross streets which ran east and west on the grid were named for native American trees, fruit trees and flowers commonly seen in that part of Texas.

Bowie Street ultimately ran all the way to the county line. As more and more cotton-related businesses were located on it and grew ever closer and closer to the gins, it took on its own personna. The businesses were lined up on both sides of Bowie going south. But they stood only one deep in most cases. Out behind them, the farmers continued to plant cotton fields on both sides of the street. The single row of buildings stretching south from Honey Oaks and surrounded by cotton fields gave the street its nickname of Cotton Row.

At 9:00 a.m. Thursday morning, two days after Slater's funeral, Clayfour parked his Dodge Ram pickup in front of the office at 2532 South Bowie and made his way towards its door. The building was stuccoed and spray painted a sandy brown color. To the left of the door on the one story tall structure were foot high aluminum numerals 2532 for the address. To the right in foot high aluminum letters was spelled out the company name, "T.J. Morgan, Cotton Production and Marketing". In the middle of the heavy oak door at eye level was a sign that stated the hours of operation for T.J. Morgan Cotton and its two after hours telephone numbers.

Clayfour glanced at his watch and calculated that the office had been open 30 minutes or so. He gripped the door handle and pushed his way inside. The main office of T.J. Morgan was a large room with various doors on the walls inside leading to storage space, bathrooms, a coffee and snack area and the private office of Morgan. In the big room were four desks of various styles and materials. The eclectic collection which also featured chairs that didn't match the desks behind which they were placed appeared to have been assembled from going to garage sales or by stealing them for little or nothing from others exiting the cotton business. A couple of metal bookshelves holding bound volumes of past transactions and stacks of ancient newspapers and magazines stood on the wall opposite the entrance. Behind the desk closest to the entrance sat a woman in her early 20's with peroxide blonde hair and a wad of chewing gum smacking continuously in her mouth.

"Good morning sir. Can I help you?", asked Donna Bradley according to the name plate on her desk.
"Is Morgan in?"

"Yes,can I tell him your name?"

"Just tell him Clayfour Peterson is here."

Donna looked up at him and asked, "Can I tell him what this is about?"

"Just say some old business, he'll know."

"Yes sir.", she said and sashayed back to his office. T.J. Morgan followed Donna out of his private office and stood defiantly glaring across the space of six feet that separated him and Clayfour at the man who had helped send him to Federal prison 10 years earlier. Clayfour and Slater had been key witnesses against him in his trial for fraud in mislabeling the quality of the bales of cotton he was exporting to a disadvantaged country that was trying to build a textile industry to give its beleaguered citizens a source of income. That he had done so under a special program sponsored by the United States Department of Agriculture which was supposed to cement good relations between the two countries, but instead had severly damaged them when his fraud was uncovered only intensified the U.S. government's desire to see him punished.

At his trial, Justin's testimony had been the most damaging to Morgan. Justin had gotten suspicious of Morgan when he had stopped hedging his cotton crops saying he no longer needed to worry about falling prices in case of a cotton surplus or the loss of his crop due to a drought or early hard freeze. Justin's father had taught him early in his career that getting the farmers of Feaster County to hedge their crops made the most economic sense. It was better for them to be able to have a steady small profit that came from hedging their crops than to experience the dramatic swings in cotton prices from year to year. Those farmers who didn't hedge went from bust to boom back to bust again with a degree of regularity that made them wonder why they had ever decided to get in the business in the first place.

So when Morgan who had been one of those smart enough to hedge suddenly declared he wouldn't need to do so anymore, it made Slater leery that Morgan had to be up to no good. In his business dealings with Morgan, Slater always thought that the cotton farmer and merchandiser had just barely run his business on the legal side of the law. If crossing the line into shady dealings would give Morgan extra profits at someone else's expense, Slater thought he was as likely to do so as not.

Clayfour had the same misgiving about Morgan. In his case, Morgan took his ginning business away from Peterson Gin after 20 years of going there. Instead, he took his cotton to be ginned to one of the newer gins, Robinson-White that had set up shop on Bowie or FCR348 as it was designated beyond the city limits 25 years ago. Already Robinson-White had gained a reputation for being willing to shade the rules if it would bring the dollars into the till. They would cheat their customers as well as help them cheat in marketing the cotton.So it made no sense to him when Morgan announced he was leaving Peterson Gin and the good service he had received there for Robinson-White unless he wanted to do something that Peterson wouldn't allow.

Their suspicions proved to be right when some of the Robinson-White hands began to brag about how they were helping to put one over on the Feds and the country where Morgan was shipping his cotton. Their tongues especially got loose after they had been paid on Thursday afternoons and spent the next six hours drinking up their paychecks at the two bars on Cotton Row heading back into Honey Oaks. Their talk began to go around Honey Oaks how Morgan was having them make bales of 80% inferior grade cotton around which they wrapped 20% high grade cotton. That made each bale appear to be all high grade cotton.

It took the braggadocio of the hands six weeks to make an impact. By then, Morgan had shipped 300 bales of the bogus cotton to the victim country. Over there, the fraud was coming undone as the managers of the textile plant who had signed on with the USDA opened the bales and found the cotton clearly not suitable for the textiles they intended to make. Back in Honey Oaks, a couple of USDA inspectors having a burger and a beer in one of the bars heard enough of the talk of the hired hands to check out what they were hearing. They started by going to see Clayfour and Justin for their input, knowing that both of them had dealt with Morgan in previous years. Justin and Clayfour had also heard the story about the ongoing scam. Their expertise in their respective fields made it easy for them to verify Morgan's duplicity. Just the fact that Morgan no longer dealt with either one of them, presumably to avoid their scrutiny of his activities was damning to him.

Soon having enough evidence for a conviction, FBI agents showed up at his office a few days later and arrested Morgan. He was brought before a Federal magistrate in Waco and charged with conspiracy to committ fraud, the fraud itself and filing false statements to cover his tracks. After his indictment, Morgan wouldn't come to trial for another nine months. That gave him time to make right his fraud. He replaced all the tainted bales rectifying that wrong. But when he came to trial, his name still wasn't totally cleared with the government. Justin and Clayfour's testimony about his business conduct and underhandedness, along with the hands who agreed to testify what they had done in exchange for leniency in settling their contribution to the misdeed, more than offset his making good on the bales. In Judge Albert Lacey's Federal courtroom, he was sunk based on the judge's reputation for being hard in giving out sentences. Mercy was not a quality that he displayed except on rare occasions. But Lacey did relent in this case and take consideration of Morgan sending the right bales at his expense. Judge Lacey had the option under the sentencing guidelines to cut Morgan some slack. Instead of the five year maximum time and the $250,000.00 fine that he could have received, Morgan was sentenced to a year at Big Spring, a low security Federal prison for low-risk offenders fairly close to Honey Oaks and a $100,000.00 fine.

Morgan did his time, paid his fine and returned to his cotton business in Honey Oaks on five years probation. He rebuilt his production and marketing business, but with a great bitterness in his heart toward those who had helped send him away. Now he snapped at Clayfour, "Peterson, what are you doing here?"

"Well, I didn't see you at Justin's funeral. I thought you would be there to spit on him when you walked past his open casket or maybe stick a pin in his hand to make sure he was dead. Unless you already knew he was gone."

"What are you insinuating? That I had something to do with his murder?" Peterson continued to look steadily at him not answering. "Well, I may have had it in for him and am glad he's gone, but I had nothing to do with what happened at Barrett Bradwell Stadium."

"How do I know that?", snapped back Clayfour.

"For one thing, I wasn't even here last Friday. I had gone to Lubbock to attend a regional cotton producers two day seminar."

"So how do we know that is for real?"

"I took my administrative assistant, Ms. Bradley with me to help gather information and go to more of the breakout meetings there." At the mention of her name, Donna blushed a crimson color like she had been caught in bed with someone else by her lover. Clayfour took note of her doing so and decided that maybe T.J. Morgan was telling the truth for once. It would be easy enough to check his story closer by contacting the people in Lubbock who hosted the seminar if need be. For now he decided to look elsewhere for who killed Justin.

CHAPTER VIII

On Sunday afternoon, Tad sat in his car in a grove of trees at Murphy Park. The grove was located on one of the higher rock outcroppings in the scenic area. It was a remote part of the park that most visitors skipped since the things that drew them there were in the more accessible parts of Murphy. The height of that part and the fact that anyone approaching it on the lone road that ended in a circle turnaround in the grove could be seen coming for quite a distance made it the perfect passion pit for the Honey Oaks High students with their raging hormones.

Tad appeared to be seated in the middle of the front seat of his pickup not quite under the steering wheel. He had a look on his face of being greatly bothered by whatever was on his mind. He moved around restlessly in his pickup. "Tarbaby, I just can't do this now. I really need to talk."

Tara Ann Reeves raised her head from Tad's lap and sat up beside him. "Hey baby, what's wrong? I know Sureshot's just not himself today." That was her pet name for Tad's penis which now lay flaccid in her left hand, his jeans and briefs down around his knees.

Tara Ann had been doing one of her favorite pastimes, giving head to the Bumblebee boys, especially the athletes. The blond junior had gotten especially good at it since she first ventured into fellatio back in the seventh grade. Then it had been heavy petting sessions, but with some of the boys begging her to "kiss it." Venturing that far led her into licking and sucking. After a couple years of practice, her lips, tongue, mouth, fingers and hands became a five piece combo that separately or in tandem made beautiful music on the boys. She could please them and tease them time and again.

The boys named her "Tarbaby" in the ninth grade. Many of them had grown up around her hearing her daddy calling her "Tara Baby" at the swimming pool, T-ball games, picnics and kindergarten classes if not before. With her initials being TAR, some of them began thinking Tarbaby when they heard her dad calling her Tara Baby. But what sealed it for them was the study of Southern American writers that the freshman English teacher, Miss Patty Barnes led in the first two six weeks periods of that school year.

Miss Barnes introduced the class to one Joel Chandler Harris of Atlanta who had amassed a collection of the stories of southern Negroes (Uncle Remus) written in their own dialects starting several years after the Civil War was over. Two of those stories really caught the imagination of her students. The first was about Brer' Fox who was always trying to catch Brer' Rabbit and cook and eat him. In his stories, Harris had the animals talking in the heavy Negro dialects to each other. Brer' Fox had finally figured out a way to catch the always elusive Brer' Rabbit who by nature was a friendly sort and expected others to treat him that way in kind. It was that trait in Brer' Rabbit that Brer' Fox saw as the Achilles heel that would allow him to catch his prey. He fashioned out of tar and turpentine a human-like figure he called a Tarbaby. Then he set it out on a path regularly traveled by Brer' Rabbit. He went into hiding nearby to see if his plan would work.

Soon enough, Brer' Rabbit came hopping down the path, noticed the Tar Baby and sang out hello. When he didn't get a response, he tried again and again. The upshot was Brer' Rabbit got madder and madder and tried punching out, kicking and butting the Tar Baby only to get hopelessly stuck. In the second story, Brer' Fox came out to say how he was going to cook and eat him. Brer' Rabbit told him he could do anything he wanted, except, "please don't throw me in that briar patch." Of course that's what Brer' Fox ended up doing and Brer' Rabbit got away because the briar patch was his home.

It didn't take the fertile imagination of the ninth grade boys long to turn Tara Ann from her daddy's Tara Baby to their own Tarbaby. And what she did when she pleasured them became known as "getting down in the briar patch.", a little ribald twist of its own. When some of them voiced it to her, she loved her nickname and their description of her act. In her sophomore year, she began to shake up the boys with a new routine. When all the kids at Honey Oaks High would gather in the cafeteria in the morning to visit before the first class bell, she would go up to a boy who she wanted for that afternoon. Staring longingly at his crotch rather than at his face, she would ask, "Suppose we get down in the briar patch at the grove after school lets out?" That boy couldn't focus on his classes at all the rest of the day as he waited for the 3:30 bell. More boys got poor daily grades because of Tarbaby than for any other reason from then on.

While the boys enjoyed watching her and the other Honeybees perform at pep rallies and on the field and court in their cute leotards and tops which in her case showed off her five-foot-eight inch figure with its 22 inch waist and 32C bust very nicely, they really liked the close up attention that she gave them. Athletes were her specialty with her act offering solace to them in defeat and the extra attention that came with the wins. Wins were the usual bill of fare for Bumblebee athletes, so her attention to them was normally a joyous occasion they were basking in accomplishing. Like the day before, Tarbaby had met the entire offensive line and its top two substitutes to reward them for taking care of Tad in the San Montevido game on Friday. They each had graded 90 or above for keeping the visitors from ever sacking Tad in the game. That performance resulted in him completing 23 of 27 passes for 387 yards and four touchdowns and rushing for 35 yards on six carries, two of those for touchdowns. San Montevido left Honey Oaks with a 56-0 pasting on its books.

That Tarbaby even knew how the offensive line had graded 90 and above in that game came because the new offensive line coach, Derrick Lindholm was someone else sampling her charms. He was a year out of Texas Tech where he had made all Southwest Conference his last two years as a Red Raider. Honey Oaks was his first job after graduation. He had noticed Tarbaby out with the Honeybees practicing their routines his first week on the job. Smitten by her and only five years older than her, Derrick hit it off almost immediately with her and soon was enjoying her as much as the Bumblebee boys did. He began to share details of the game like game grades of the linemen that he was responsible for with Tarbaby. That kind of information made her even better at what she enjoyed doing for and to the boys. Coach Lindholm was in lust if not in love with her.

Tara Ann looked steadily into Tad's eyes. A warm sympathetic smile was on her face. "Well it must be pretty heavy if you're not responding to what I'm doing. So what's on your mind?"

Tad gazed right back as intently and earnestly as she had ever seen him do. "Last week when Justin was killed."

"Un huh"

"I saw something that has really been bothering me. Matter of fact, that's just one of the two things that I've seen the last few months that are really getting to me."

"What are they Tad?"

"You got to promise to say nothing to nobody if I tell you."

"Hey sweetie, we've been friends a long time. I wouldn't let you down by talking."

"You sure?"

"Absolutely hon, have you ever doubted me?"

"Well no, but these are really big."

"I sure can't say anything if I don't know what your big secrets are.", laughed Tara. "So get a load off."

"Well okay, here goes, but you've promised."

Tad started with that early July midday trip to his house which seemed to have changed his life forever. He recounted how before that day, it had been his hope his mother and dad would get back together. That his dad would move back home and his mother would drop her petition for divorce. Then he moved forward to his boss sending him home to get his safety helmet before driving the fork lift. Tad's eyes glistened with tears as he said, "Tara, Mom was supposed to be in Dallas seeing my aunt that day. I thought that no one was home. But then I heard a noise from their bedroom of people laughing and talking quietly."

Tara's eyes were wide with wonder and sympathy as Tad poured out his story." When I got close to the room, the door was open just wide enough so that I coud see into the room. God, Tara, it was awful!"

"Tad what was it?" implored Tarbaby.

"It was my mom and Justin Slater in there and they both were naked. Her back was to me and he was facing me. He had his hands on her boobs. She had one hand on his cheek. But the other was holding his prick, kinda' like you're holding mine."

"Well, I haven't totally forgotten what we're here for.", responded Tara as her left hand made a caressing motion on him.

"Yeah, but Tara, he was real hard! Then he told mom he wanted to go in her and guess what happened?"

"What Tad?"

"They were in the middle of the room when he said that and Mom grabbed onto his hard-on firmly and used it to guide him to the bed. She fell back onto it and pulled him down on top of her."

"Wow!", exclaimed Tara. "So did they fuck?"

"I don't know!", cried Tad. "I guess they did. I couldn't stand the idea of Justin fucking Mom, so I ran off."

"Did they know you were there?"

"No, I was very quiet leaving the house."

Tad went on, "Anyway from that day on, I hated Justin feeling he had ruined it for my dad to get back home."

Tara Ann asked, "Is that why you missed out on the Booster Club Golf and Tennis Extravaganza and the annual hamburger feed?"

"Yes, the less I saw Justin, the better off I would be was what I was feeling."

"Why Tad!", she exlaimed, "if people knew what had happened and how it made you feel, they might think it was you that killed Justin."

"I know.", he replied. "But I never would have done that. You've known me long enough Tarbaby to know that's not me."

"Yes that's true, but still Tad, Sheriff Gumby hasn't arrested anyone yet."

"That brings me to the second thing I saw which has bothered me even more."

"What would that be?", queried Tara, her face now covered with a frown that had displaced the smile with which she had started this conversation. Tad began to talk about what he saw the day Justin was killed. He was very relieved to finally be able to talk about both these issues which had been pressuring him.

"A week ago Friday when we were going to play Turnersborough, I went to the stadium about three o'clock. I was feeling some soreness in my right elbow like maybe it was strained. I told our new trainer, Mr. Carlisle about it that morning. He told me to ice it down for a while in the training room. He said he would have a tub of ice waiting for me which he did."

"Well go on Tad.", urged Tara very anxious to find out what he had seen.

He continued, "After I finished icing my elbow, I came up the stairs all the way to the press box. I decided to stop there and see if the game programs were printed and distributed yet."

"That wasn't what got to you Tad. Go ahead. Tell me now!"

"First of all Tara, I saw Slater coming into the stadium with his money bags. He made a beeline for the Bee Hive with them. I watched him go inside and close the door. The game programs were there okay so I began reading one of them."

Totally exasperated with Tad by now, Tara Ann said in frustration, "So was that all you saw?"

He looked back at her and said softly, "No it wasn't. A couple of minutes later, I sensed someone else was walking toward the Bee Hive. I looked up and saw it was Coach Donaldson."

"What happened then?"

"I don't know. I saw him go into the Bee Hive and shut the door. I left the press box and went on home to do a few things before I had to report back here at 5:00. It was about the time that I got back here when our moms found Justin murdered."

Tara Ann mouthed her second "Wow!" of their talk on hearing Tad's account. "So do you think that Coach Donaldson had it in for Justin? Could he even have done that so brutally?"

"He certainly has the size and strength to have buried that Stinger Sticker deep into his chest. But why he would, I don't know."

"Why have you kept this secret for so long?"

"I don't know Tarbaby. That game was about to happen and the Bumblebees already had a lot on their plates to handle. I decided to wait."

"Tad, you've got to talk to someone in authority about what you saw. Honey Oaks High and the town are still real spooked that Justin could get killed in broad daylight in such a public place and nobody get arrested for it."

"I know.", Tad replied. "I am trying to figure out who I want to tell, our principal, Mr. Rasco or Sheriff Gumby. I'll go to one of them tomorrow and tell what I saw."

When he said that, Tara Ann could feel the tension go out of his body for the first time since they had arrived in the grove. He drew in a deep gulp of air and relaxed. It was as if the proverbial yoke had been removed from his neck when he shared his secrets with Tarbaby. Meantime her left hand had stayed in place holding him the whole time he talked. She had continued to occasionally stroke him throughout their talk. So as the rest of his body went into a state of relaxation, that was not the case with Sureshot. It was as big and as firm as ever in her clasp. Taking notice of this, she turned to Tad and said, "I see that our talk cleared the air. We're back to why we came here." With that Tarbaby ducked her head and went back down into the briar patch.

CHAPTER IX

Thompson Brothers Investments branch office in Honey Oaks was located at the corner of Lamar and Pecan Streets three blocks southeast of the Feaster County Courthouse. It fronted on Lamar with its entrance right on the sidewalk. It was in a four story office building which had been built in the first wave of commercial growth following the end of World War II. The building had been remodeled and updated several times since then. The last time had been in 1987 after its current owners had bought it for a song from the Resolution Trust Corporation. RTC had acquired ownership in it when the previous owners had taken bankruptcy early in 1986 when the credit and real estate markets crumbled in wave after wave of failed overinflated and underfinanced property transactions.

The new owners had offered Thompson Brothers and Justin Slater a sweetheart lease including a lot of special buildouts to become the primary ground floor tenant. It had been too good to turn down. Especially when the new owners bought the run-down building next door and razed it for a parking lot. The lot gave the clients of Thompson Brothers easy access to off-street parking. On Monday morning, Clayfour eased his pickup into a parking space that abutted the building. It was 8:15 a.m., just enough time for him to get a cup of coffee, check the markets and join the sweaters in the bullpen. At 8:30 a.m trading would begin in both the commodity and stock markets.

Clayfour poured himself a cup of straight black coffee into a porcelain mug which was emblazoned with the Thompson Brothers Investments logo, TBI, set in the middle of a colorful crest and shield. Using those mugs instead of styrofoam cups had been the brainchild of Barton Slater. It made the clients feel that much more special when they drank from them. Clayfour greeted several of the regulars who were fixing their coffee to their own preferences as he made his way through them and toward a row of chairs that faced the electronic board. The board was spewing routine announcements out in bright orange lights onto its face. Five minutes from now, the lights would begin to spew out stock symbols and their appropriate prices and net changes unabated for the next six and a half hours.

Peterson was clad in jeans, a blue short sleeve pima cotton work shirt and brown Wolverine work boots. From the pocket of his work shirt, he took out a small notebook and a ball point pen which the Peterson Gin Company gave away to its customers. It gave him the appearance of getting ready to track the market, But in reality, it was a guise to allow him to sit close to Doctor Chuck McGuire. McGuire was a tenured agri-business professor with nearly 35 years on the faculty at Tarleton State University. Clayfour had been in two of his classes before he dropped out of school to become a city cop some 30 years earlier. McGuire was in his late 50's and carried about 40 extra pounds on his five-foot-eight-inch frame. He had a Roman nose that tapered off sharply about half way down plastering it flat against his face. He wore big black horned rim spectacles. He had thin wisps of gray hair that clung to his otherwise bald head as if each strand knew its days were numbered. Taken together, the nose and the spectacles reminded his students of a wise old owl. Accordingly, they called him Hootie. Hootie wore a standard uniform of a gray corduroy jacket with black leather patches, a white oxford cloth shirt with a button down collar and Wrangler Jeans over which his ample gut protruded. He always had on half quarter work boots as if he would have to lead his classes into a field, feed lot or pasture at any moment. But the truth was Hootie was only seen by his students in the classroom nowadays.

He usually spent his mornings on Monday, Wednesday and Friday at Thompson Brothers from just before the markets opened until around 11:00 a.m. He was there on Tuesdays and Thursdays from right after lunch until about 30 minutes after the market closed, about 3:30 p.m. That he could even be at the market to buy and sell stocks and bonds was a story in itself. For he had lost everything including his home 10 years earlier when his call on the direction of the July wheat futures contracts proved to be the opposite of where they eventually settled when the contract expired. So sure was he of his hunch about wheat prices that he had given one of his agri-business classes an assignment to gather information from the growers, millers and bankers who financed their operations about their opinion of the direction of the market. The assignment had been a ruse to to find out if those in the business felt the same way he did about the direction of the wheat crop prices.

His students had called on people in the wheat trade in the Texas Panhandle and further north into Oklahoma and Kansas. What they learned convinced him that wheat was headed to higher prices not seen since the Arab oil embargo days of 1973. Hootie had Justin start buying him the 5000 bushel contracts for delivery the next July in October the year before. Initially his strategy worked as July wheat climbed 10 cents a bushel. Hootie used the extra buying power created by his paper profits to add to his positions staying leveraged on 10% equity to the max.

One of the factors that had helped him build the immense paper profits was a drought that had started in August and continued on unceasingly. The long range weather forecasts indicated it was not about to end. Wheat kept going up as a result and Hootie kept building his position. Then Mother Nature played a cruel joke and sent the rains in drought—busting intensity beginning in mid February. The more it rained, the better the prospects for a bumper wheat crop that summer. The monthly USDA crop reports began to project harvests to be much higher than Hootie and many others had thought. Speculators and hedgers alike began to change their positions and sell off the July and the following months futures contracts. Prices were dropping now as fast as they had been going up just a month earlier.

Hootie couldn't believe what was happening so sure was he of his information being right. He just knew that the rains would end and prices would begin to head back up again. But the margin clerks at Thompson Brothers Investments who were seeing his equity and his profits drop almost daily took a more practical view and asked him to put up additional margin or sell some of his positions nearly every day. Hootie cleaned out every saving and retirement account that he had accumulated in his 25 years at TSU to meet the calls and hang on to most of his position. Slater had known him to be a good client over the years and continued to work with him, though he was getting irrational in his thought processes as his life's savings were tumbling down the streams that came with each additional rainfall. Hootie decided to do short term trades in a number of commodities and try to take short term profits to bolster his position. He would stand by the quote machine out in the bullpen for the use of the sweaters and check prices almost minute by minute of silver, pork bellies, lumber and other commodities that had sharper than normal price movements taking place. He irritated some of the sweaters by his hogging the machine as he made trades. The trades he asked for showed how hopeless his situation had become. Hootie would yell out to Justin in his private office to "Buy 10 May silvers!" then a second later, "No!, sell them!"He was at sea in a subject he was supposed to be an expert in.

The July wheat contract expired 20 cents a bushel lower than the price had been when Hootie had first started buying nine months earlier. Hootie was a ruined man. Thompson Brothers had been forced to liquidate his positions against his will when there was no more equity left and no more money to put in. He had mortgaged his home which had been paid off the last five years to get one last round of funds to carry out his dreams, no, pipedreams. The house had to be sold to take care of the mortgage. Hootie still had his tenured job and didn't have to declare bankruptcy as he could pay off all that he had obligated himself for, but there was nothing left. He had pleaded with Justin for Thompson Brothers to go along with him and not liquidate his speculations. Justin had to explain that rules were rules and there was nothing he could do about it.

Hootie was very angry at Justin and Thompson Brothers blaming them for his turn of events more than he did himself. Some days the words between him and Justin got very strong and he was asked to leave the office. Around Honey Oaks and at the Tarleton State campus, he bemoaned his situation with bitter words saying that he wouldn't have been in that situation but for the actions of Justin and Thompson Brothers Investments. He even with a show of biting humor threatened to write a book about his experiences to warn other commodity speculators about the dangers of making trades like that. There came a period of several years that he was never seen at Justin's office since he had no money to do anything anyway.

Gradually he saved some money and worked his way out of being on the bottom. He got to where he wanted to invest some in the stock market and went in to talk to Justin about doing so. It had been a heart to heart talk between the two of them with Justin saying he needed an apology for Hootie badmouthing him all over the area. Hootie grudgingly gave him that. Justin told him that there would be no commodity trading allowed and no stock or bond purchases on anything but a cash basis if he wanted to reopen an account there. Hootie agreed to the terms and began making small purchases of stock. For the most part he no longer talked down Justin to anyone, except just every once in a while, a jab would come out when he lectured a class about hedging crops.

Clayfour had known about the earlier situation that brought Hootie down as did everyone else who frequented the Thompson Brothers office. His thought that perhaps Hootie might still have it in for Justin came from hearing comments from some of the students he hired for part time jobs during ginning season talking about Hootie making comments in class that indicated Justin might still be a thorn in his side.

Clayfour moved to an empty chair beside Hootie who out of habit had seated himself as close to the quote machine as he could. "Morning Hootie. How's it going today?"

"So far, so good. The markets's still two minutes from opening.", quipped Hootie. "Ask me again in 15 minutes."

"I'm curious. What's worth owning now?"

"I'm putting my money in some grain processing stocks that can convert the raw plants into ethanol. As we use up our oil supplies, I think we'll look for alternate fuels to burn, like ethanol.", said Hootie earnestly.

Clayfour shifted in his chair and replied, "I was wondering. I hadn't seen you since Justin's funeral. You went by his casket close to where I was sitting with the other pall bearers."

"Yeah, that's right. I saw you out of the corner of my eye as I walked by."

"Poor Justin. Were you surprised that someone so brutally murdered him?"

"You know Clayfour, probably not. In his business when people have their money or their livelihoods on the line with him, I'm not surprised that he got somebody mad enough to do him in."

Clayfour's gaze was zeroed in on Hootie's face as if his flat nose against his cheeks was a blip on a radar screen."So speaking of that, what about you Hootie? I hear from the kids I hire at the gin who are in your classes that your experiences here on that wheat deal are still pretty close to being raw on your nerves.Would you still have been mad enough after all these years to have gone to Barrett Bramwell and stabbed him like that nearly two weeks ago?"

Hootie's face reddened and he hissed under his breath to Clayfour, "I was pretty mad at him for what happened back then. And yeah, I still say something to my classes from time to time that he and Thompson Brothers did me dirty when wheat started falling. And I probably said over the last 10 years I wish that he was dead. But to actually kill him? No! There's no way I would have been able to do that. Besides in looking back, I was as much at fault because I got greedy and went crazy buying on margin. That's when I was trying to make a killing. Not now, even if I do say things to my classes."

Clayfour looked away and glanced up at the board which was beginning to show the first trades of the day. Momentarily the effect on him was hypnotic as it was for the dozen or so sweaters who would stay there all day, save for a quick lunch at the deli down the hall from Thompson Brothers and bathroom and coffee breaks, until the market had run its course for the day. But Clayfour was gathering his thoughts as he watched the tape and got back to the conversation. "Well maybe so Hootie. But you ought to keep any negative thoughts about Justin to yourself. Gumby is still chasing down leads. And you're one that it's well known you could have had the motive. And there's still another thing to consider."

"What would that be Clayfour?"

"It was two Fridays ago when Justin was killed. Don't you have MWF classes in Stephenville?"

"Yes I do. I teach at 1:00 p.m. and again at 3:00 p.m.those days. One hour classes each time."

"So you wouldn't have been here in Honey Oaks when Justin got killed?"

"Exactly, I have a class that gets out around four. Then usually a student or two hangs around to ask about his or her work or an upcoming test or assignment for 15 or 20 minutes."

"That all sounds good and fine Hootie, but there's one thing I remember from when I was in your class 30 years ago."

With his eyes narrowing to where they appeared half-closed behind his spectacles, Hootie asked defensively, "Oh yeah, what was that?"

"I had a MWF afternoon class with you both times I took courses from you.They were both fall semester classes. Your nephew Allan was playing fullback for the Bumblebees and making quite a name for himself on the football field. He made varsity as a sophomore when I was a senior tight end and was he good. His senior year when I was at Tarleton, he rushed for over 1800 yards and 27 or 28 touchdowns as the Bumblebees went 12-1 losing out in the regional semi-finals. Being his uncle and a big Honey Oaks High fan anyway, you were just as likely to give your last Friday afternoon class a walk on a game day so that you could get to the game at home or away in plenty of time. I still remember getting out early on those Fridays. Do you do it any differently now?"

When Hootie began to sputter as he tried to answer the question, Clayfour knew that the students in the 3:00 p.m. Friday class of Agriculture Finance 201 had not met for class the day Justin died. So if Hootie wasn't in class an hour or so away from Honey Oaks then, where was he? Clayfour saw that Hootie was agitated enough that this pretense at a casual conversation was over. To press the issue any further would blow the cover under which he was trying to help Dalton Gumby with the case. There were still others at Thompson Brothers he wanted to check out. So he got up, turned towards Hootie and said, "Hey, it was just what I remembered. Don't let it upset your day. I've got to get to the gin. See you later." As Clayfour then turned to head towards the coffee bar carrying his mug to pour out and put into the sink, Hootie managed to get out a strangled goodbye. He was trying to act cool as if nothing had happened, but Clayfour knew his comments had struck a chord in Hootie he didn't want showing.

CHAPTER X

Clayfour climbed back into his pickup and drove south on Bowie Street til he reached the Peterson Gin Company. Parking in his reserved spot close to the front porch, he walked through the door marked "Office". His secretary of 15 years, Diana Magness gave him a big smile, "Hello Boss. You're running late today."

"I had to make an early stop at Thompson Brothers to check some things. I stayed longer than I had planned. Now I've got to get busy."

"Here's your phone calls to return and your mail." Diana handed two small handfuls of pink message sheets and letters and catalogues to him.

"Thanks Diana, I'll get on these now." He started towards his office door, then turned back to her., "Get Dalton Gumby on the phone for me."

"Sure Clayfour, I'm dialing now. I'll put him right through if he's there."

Clayfour had just gotten seated comfortably in his big executive leather chair when his phone rang. "Dalton's on the line Clayfour."

"Okay, thanks Diana." He pushed line one that was blinking and connected, "Hey Dalton, how's it going?"

"Clayfour, it's slow. Some phone calls, but nothing of consequence. What about you?"

"Dalton I have a couple of leads I'm following. Suppose we have some ribs out at Danny's Ribs 'n More about 11:30 and I'll fill you in. If we're that early, we can grab that outdoor table that's set off by itself and talk quietly with no one hearing us."

"Sounds good, I'll see you then and I'm buying."

"You don't have to do that."

"Hey, it's the least I can do. Just bring your appetite and your info, of course."

By 11:00 Clayfour had returned all his calls and gone through his mail. He had studied some inventory lists of ginning supplies that had been prepared by his managers and saw about five items that needed to be replenished before ginning season started. If the weather followed its normal pattern, the first freeze that kicked off the ginning operations would be six weeks away. But Clayfour knew how fickle Texas weather was and that the first freeze might come as early as three weeks out. Accordingly, he got on the phone to three different suppliers and arranged for those items to be at Peterson Gin two weeks from now. That done, he rushed past Diana saying, "I'm gone to lunch."

"So soon? Boy, it must be nice to be the boss. I'd like to go to lunch now.", joshed Diana kiddingly. Their 15 years together running Peterson Gin made their relationship more of equals rather than boss-secretary. Clayfour had no problem having Diana wise off about him.

"Dalton said he would buy me ribs at Danny's if I could meet him out there at 11:30. I'm not turning that down even if you think it's too early. See you after one." Clayfour climbed back into his truck and headed east toward Danny's.

When Dalton arrived, he saw that Clayfour had beat him there and staked out the table they wanted. He headed that way followed by a young waitress. Sitting down, he greeted Clayfour, "I guess you must be hungry beating me here like this."

Before Clayfour could respond, Pam the young waitress, a local girl a year or so out of high school, jumped in and said, "What would you all like to drink?"

Dalton answered, "Sweet teas for both of us. And bring us the big platter of ribs and two plates."

"Whoa Dalton, I can't eat that much.", interjected Clayfour. "As much as I love ribs, my system won't allow me to eat more than two or three."

Dalton responded, "It's no problem. I can eat a bunch of them and take the rest home." He turned to Pam who hovered over them, pencil and pad in hand, unsure what she was supposed to do. "Hon, go ahead just like I told you. And hurry!, we both have other things to do." She hustled off heading towards the kitchen and drink station to put in their order.

"That was spoken by a man 10 years younger, 60 pounds lighter and seven inches shorter with the metabolism of a frisky young colt. Two or three will definitely do me. And then I may need a quick nap to make it"., retorted Clayfour with a big grin on his face. He continued, "But you're a legend around here, the sheriff with the bottomless pit for a stomach."

Gumby grinned back at him, "I do like my ribs. But before she gets back with them, tell me what you have so far." Clayfour related to him his suspicions about T.J. Malone and Hootie McGuire, their past problems with Justin that caused him to focus on them first and his encounters with them since the funeral.

He said,"I think, based on how red the face of T.J.'s secretary, Donna Bradley got when he mentioned being in Lubbock at a cotton producers seminar two Fridays ago that he's going to have a solid alibi. I just need to verify it which I can do with the Lubbock people who put on the seminar."

Dalton looked a little puzzled, "What does his secretary's red face have to do with it."

"Donna Bradley? Have you seen her? She's providing T. J. more than secretarial services. Anyway he said she was on the trip with him when I challenged him about being in Lubbock. Supposedly to attend some seminar sessions that overlapped others he wanted to attend. That's when her face went so red, when he was telling it. She blushes real pretty."

"What about Hootie?"

"When we sat together this morning at Thompson Brothers and talked, I reminded him that when I took a couple of courses from him 30 years ago, he was such a Bumblebee fan with his brother's son Allan Jr. starring for a typically great Honey Oaks team and how he used to give his classes that met on mid Friday afternoons walks on game days. Based on how he reacted to that, I'd say that his late Friday class when Justin died got a walk also."

Dalton asked,"So would that have given him enough time to have made it to Barrett Bradwell and killed Justin?"

"It's a possibility. I'm going to pry around discretely and see what I can find."

A tray balanced expertly on her right shoulder, Pam returned with their order She lowered the tray and set their glasses of tea in front of them. Between them she set down a big platter covered with two dozen ribs, meaty, steaming hot and dripping in the sweet sauce which had been added to them by Danny after he had first smoked them for over 12 hours. The ribs set in the pit away from the coals for another hour or so to let the sauce soak in and make the meat on them so tender it fell apart when someone picked them up to begin eating. To complete the order, Pam set out a plate with slices of white bread to sop up the sauce that dripped on the platter or to use as napkins to wipe their hands of the sauce and then be eaten as a treat. The table also had a roll of paper towels and a bowl filled with packages of wet towelettes for the customers who wanted to eat in a more civilized manner. Everything dispersed from her tray, Pam asked, "Can I get you anything else?"

Clayfour and Dalton both answered at the same time, "No, we're good to go." Then they both put some ribs on their individual plates and began to eat.

True to his word and metabolism, Dalton polished off a dozen ribs in the next 45 minutes. The ribs were so good that Clayfour stuffed down four of them figuring that he could nap some in his office to make up for his gluttony. When neither one could find room for any more ribs to go down, Dalton waved at Pam and hollered, "Hon, can you bring me a to go box for the rest of these? Here's for the bill and here's something for you." He handed her a $5.00 bill as a tip in addition to the money for the bill. "Oh, by the way, bring me a receipt too." Turning to Clayfour, he asked, "So what are you doing next?"

Clayfour answered, "Getting a nap in first." Then he got serious," The Booster Club is having its first meeting tonight since Justin died. There may be something I can learn there. A lot of people will show up to give their support not only for what's already happened, but also for Friday's game. It'll be in the Metroplex at Colleyville Southside. That school's growing real fast and just moved up from 3A to 4A. It has a couple of Divison I prospects."

Gumby said, "Sounds interesting. If I get a chance, I might come by."

"That'll be great. Thanks for the ribs. Maybe I'll see you there tonight."

CHAPTER XI

Though the Booster Club meeting wouldn't start until 6:30, Clayfour arrived 20 minutes early and walked into Barrett Bradwell Stadium. He looked down on the field to see the Bumblebee varsity and junior varsity teams practicing on the artificial surface. The quarterbacks, running backs and receivers were running drills about the 10 yard line on the north end of the field. The offensive line did blocking drills time and again at the 45 yard line. On the other 45 yard line, linebackers and defensive backs were gathered to hear instructions about the plans they would be using against Colleyville Southside Friday. At the 30 were grouped the defensive linemen working against each other to penetrate offensive lines. At the 15,six players were lined up in two groups of three. It was the Bumblebee kickers, Eldon Brewer and Sean McAllister who were practicing field goals once their snappers got the ball centered back to the holders. Two players stood behind the goal post to catch the kicks and get the ball back to the snappers.

Clayfour's attention was caught by the sight of 16 girls in shorts, team shirts and tennis shoes high kicking in unison on the running track on the south side of the field. He could make out the music the Honeybees were practicing to for the new dance routine they would be debuting on the road at Colleyville Southside Friday. Clayfour noted how Leslie Reeves rehearsed the Honeybees, stopping the music frequently to go back over a step she thought the dance group was missing. As always, Leslie brooked no imperfection from the Honeybees.

Coach Matt Donaldson blew his whistle, a signal for all the team members of both squads to come together in the center of the field. They stood on the Honey

Oaks crest that was on the 50 yard line. The crest had a gold outer circle, a black inner circle in which the letters "H-O" stood out in the same gold color as the outer circle. A bumblebee with its stinger out was inside the letters. Practice was done. Donaldson complimented the teams on having a good Monday session and let them know what they would work on Tuesday. Meantime Reeves had dismissed the Honeybees. The girls had to run down the track to their dressing room past the football teams. Their movement in the form-clinging outfits distracted a few of the players who looked their way too long. A quick rebuke by their names from Donaldson brought them back in line. Finally it was over. The teams raised hands joining them together in one show of solidarity yelling, "Bumblebees! Yes! Bzzz!" Then they broke for their locker room. Clayfour headed towards the Bee Hive.

A man wearing a Honey Oaks ISD maintenance uniform stepped out in front of him about 50 yards from the Bee Hive. "Hello Clayfour, long time, no see." Clayfour looked at him closer, realizing it was someone he had gone to school with, but no name came to him now. "Jerry Schilling. I graduated with you.", said the short balding man as he offered his hand to Clayfour.

Clayfour shook with him saying," Jerry! Of course! But I haven't seen you around here in a long time."

"No. I joined the Army two weeks after we graduated. Stayed in it for three hitches Then I met my wife in Indiana close to where I had been stationed. I married her and got a job with a metal fabrication company in Illinois. I was there a few years. Mom had to go into a rest home the first of June. My sisters all live away from here with their families. I've been divorced for 10 years with no kids. So I was the logical one to come home and help out with Mom. This job was open when I arrived. So here I am."

"Well, I'm out at the cotton gin. We'll have to get together. I need to get in there." Clayfour gestured towards the Bee Hive. "It's good to see you again Jerry."

Inside the Bee Hive, it was literally a buzz of activity as a full house of Bumblebee parents and grandparents, exes and other fans occupied every chair and stood against the walls waiting for the meeting to begin. Leslie Reeves had come inside and stood up at the front table talking with Kim Whittaker and several of the other Booster Club officers. Tara Ann came in shortly after and went up to her mom. "Mom, I am going to go get a burger with Sharon and Dana. Can you give me some money?"

"Well, I don't have much with me. I had prepared a roast with all the veggies this afternoon. I thought we could have that."

"Oh please Mom, I'm not that hungry. Besides we have a chemistry test tomorrow. Sharon and Dana and I are going to go over our notes together at Dana's."

"I suppose so, but this is all I can give you.", she said as she fished a $10.00 bill out of her pocket.

"Thanks Mom.",she said as she headed toward the door. She bumped into Tad who was coming in to hit Kim up for some eating money also. She asked him, "Did you contact Mr Rasco yet?"

"No, I had some meetings I had to take care of. I will do it in the morning."

The exchange between Leslie and Tara Ann was noted by two moms of football players sitting back on the third row. "That Tara Ann is really cute.", said Monica Robinson whose son Ryan was the starting center for the Bumblebees.

"That's for sure.", replied Amy McCloud whose son Arnold lined up at right guard beside Ryan. "She is a stunner. But there's something about her that has me puzzled."

"What about her?", queried Monica.

"Well, Arnold sometimes calls her Tarbaby instead of Tara Ann."

"I know. So does Ryan. When I asked him why, he just giggles and walks off."

"That sounds just like what Arnold does. I wonder why they call her Tarbaby."

"I don't know, but just the other day, Saturday I think, I heard Arnold talking on the phone about going down in the briar patch. They've really gotten into Uncle Remus ever since studying about Joel Chandler Harris in the ninth grade."

Monica came back, "You never know what they're going to come up with next. We'll probably never know what this Tarbaby—briar patch stuff is all about. Kids are crazy sometimes in what they get attached to."

A voice from the front table brought their attention back to the meeting. It was the vice-president of the Bumblebee Booster Club, Tibby Foster. She was opening the meeting, a job that for the past two plus years had been carried out by Justin Slater. Now according to the bylaws of the club, Tibby had become the president until elections were held at the last meeting of the school year, usually in April the next year. Tibby was a tall slender woman with a ready smile that would break out at any moment. She kept her hair in a close cut pageboy and wore glasses that enhanced the perpetual pleasant expression on her face. Unlike

Justin whose children were graduated from the Honey Oaks ISD, Tibby's daughter Jennifer was a sophomore starter on the varsity volleyball team. Possessed of her mother's height, Jennifer was a middle blocker on the defending district champion team. Behind her were two more Fosters, Lee in the eighth grade and Josie in the sixth grade. Tibby would be a Booster Club member for quite a spell before the last of the Fosters graduated from Honey Oaks High.

Tibby said, "I welcome all of you to this first meeting of the Booster Club since Justin's tragic death. Let's all take a moment of silence to honor his memory and all he did for this club. Please stand." The audience rose as one. Most of its members bowed their heads in reverent silence. But some of them were staring at the spot on the floor where Justin had been found skewered by the Stinger Sticker. While most of the blood stains had been taken up, it was still possible to see some traces of where Justin had laid in a pool of his own blood. There was some visible shuddering and cries of sorrow throughout the crowd. Tibby let the moment go a little longer, then said, "Thank you and be seated. We need to move ahead. Let's begin with the treasurer's report Kim." Kim walked to the stand carrying a single sheet of paper.

Looking over the crowd, she began, "I guess the big thing is the income we anticipated getting from the Turnersborough game that didn't materialize. The San Montevido game brought us about what was expected, maybe even more since there was a bigger crowd, possibly drawn here by Justin's slaying much as I hate to say it, but just to be blunt about it."

"So what do the numbers look like Kim?", said Tibby asking the question that was uppermost in the minds of most of the crowd.

Kim glanced down at the sheet in her hand. "After Friday, we have $27,534.72 in the bank. Had Turnersborough happened, it would have been more like $35,000.00 plus. Making it up is going to be a real challenge the rest of the year."

In the audience, Jerry Carrothers raised his hand and asked, "What if we don't? What happens then?"

Kim who pulled no punches in laying it on the line responded, "Jerry, we would just have to cut our budget if the money's not there. Maybe we don't give as many scholarships next May as we did this past May." That remark started a buzz of unhappy conversation particularly among the parents of seniors who were hoping to see their children get a scholarship from the club. As their remarks grew louder, words condemning Dalton Gumby for making Barrett Bradwell totally a crime scene could be heard. As if somehow the sheriff was to blame for the shortfall. Tibby took back the rostrum from Kim. She held up her hand to signal for the crowd to be quiet. There was an immediate hush throughout the Bee Hive as everyone followed Tibby's lead.

She spoke up firmly, "Hey everybody, nothing's happened yet and maybe it won't. Our board's not even had a chance to meet yet since Justin's death. Believe me we're aware of this and will come up with a plan. But Kim's right. If the income doesn't come up to what we budgeted, we'll have to cut expenses. I know that's painful to hear, but we'll get back to you as quickly as possible." Her calm reassuring manner had quieted the crowd.

She continued, "We're on a tight schedule. And I know you'll want to hear from Coach Donaldson and see the San Montevido game. So we'll move quickly with announcements. First, we've filled two buses so far to go the Colleyville Southside game. The third bus still has a lot of seats available. We need to have all reservations by Thursday morning before noon."

"What's it cost again and when do the buses go there?", came a voice from the audience.

"It costs $35.00 a person, $30.00 for students and younger children. That includes a ticket to the game, snacks coming and going and a meal after the game, maybe with the team. The buses leave at 3:15 sharp Friday. Any children going will be excused from their classes at 3:00 to make it to the buses here at Barrett Bradwell before the 3:15 departure."

"If there's a need, can we get a fourth bus?"

Tibby answered, "Possibly, but we would have to have the third one filled by noon tomorrow. Come back to Kim with your reservations. Now let's talk about the volleyball match there. Our junior varsity and varsity play Southside there at 4:00 and 5:15 Friday. The bus carrying them will leave at 12:30. Coach Harwell has our varsity really playing well. We've lost only one match this year. We hope a bunch of you will make it up there to yell for the Lady Bees before the football game at 7:30. Any other announcements?"

Tibby waited a moment. When no one else spoke up, she announced, "Here's what we've all been waiting for. Coach Donaldson will report on last Friday's game and then tell us about Colleyville Southside before we look at the San Montevido game film. Coach Donaldson, come on up." Matt Donaldson had been leaning against the back wall waiting for this time. Still in his coaching sweats and leather athletic shoes, he strode quickly to the front. He was greeted by lots of clapping and yelling from the enthusiastic crowd.

"Thanks to all of you. Boy!, what a difference a week makes. Last Friday was vintage Bumblebee football." The crowd erupted again hollering and shouting at Donaldson's pronouncement. He raised his hand for quiet and went on, "The boys might well have played their best game in the last three years beating San Montevido. I believe when you see the game film, you'll see what I'm talking about. But there's one person here tonight who deserves most of the credit for our win. That would be our new line coach, Derrick Lindholm. In case you didn't notice it, our offensive line kept the San Montevido defense away from Tad. He went 23 for 27 with no interceptions for 345 yards and no interceptions. He had some pretty good rushing numbers too. For that we can thank Coach Lindholm and how he continues to make the offensive line better and better each week. Derrick, why don't you come on up and tell us how you did it."

The young ex-Red Raider only five years older than his senior linemen bounced up to the front. The six-foot-six-inch, 280-pound—All SWC tackle had a big smile on his face as he went through the lines of people clapping him up to the front. He waited on them to settle down and began to talk in his west Texas twang he had acquired growing up in Petersburg. "Thank you all, but it's the kids you need to be cheering. I just showed them the blocking schemes. They carried them out and did so mighty good by the way. Do you know that seven of them, our five starters and the top two subs, Gardner and Lincoln, all graded at least 90 for the game. We never did have a game like that at Tech where so many graded so high. You can be proud of your kids."

"Hey Coach! Will they do that again Friday at Colleyville?"

"I am working on some slightly different schemes to combat their sending two linebackers on nearly every play. Those are their two Divison I prospects. They don't both come on each play, but there's usually at least one coming each play. They're good at penetrating into the offensive backfield of their opponents. That's what we're working to stop them from doing in our practices this week."

Tibby interrupted and said, "If there's no more questions for Coach Lindholm, we need to get to the film. It's a short night for us tonight as there's a senior parents meeting at 8:30 inside the library." No one said anything, but politely clapped for Lindholm as he went back to stand by Coach Donaldson. The big screen on the side wall came down and the lights dimmed. Everyone turned their chairs to watch the film with Donaldson narrating the action on the screen. He made frequent stops and rewound the film so that the fans could see in detail what his expert eyes were seeing as the plays unfolded. Finally it was over at 8:15 and the members filed out of the Bee Hive to either go home or to the school library. Clayfour was one of the last to leave wondering if his time had been wasted in learning more about Justin's killing. At least it had been great to once more be at a Honey Oaks Booster Club meeting.

CHAPTER XII

Tad didn't go see his principal Leon Rasco until midway through the third period. Instead he had spent the time with his two wide receivers Desmond and Larry at Murphy Park working on his passing game with them. Just doing that had been a form of therapy for him to spend time in that pretty setting flinging footballs to his two close friends and teammates. He had felt a need for being in that setting especially hard the last few days. While telling Tara Ann what he had seen and vowing to her to report it had lifted his burden in one way, it had increased it in other ways as the hour of reckoning drew nearer. He had slept less and less each night. It seemed that after having pizza out last night with five of his teammates after he got the money from Kim to do so, he had not had a minute of sleep. Instead he had stared at the face of his alarm clock all through the night. The minutes had crept by even slower. To Tad each minute seemed to be reluctant to cede its time glowing in the dark on the clock face. Instead each one seemed to have managed to stretch its stay on the face an extra two minutes or so before giving way to the next number.

He had fallen into an exhaustion-induced stupor around 5:00 a.m. It took Kim yelling at him every two minutes or so to wake up at 7:30 to bring him around. She had gotten her real estate license since Robert had moved out to try to make some extra money and fill the lonely hours while Tad was in school. Her broker always held a 8:00 a.m. Tuesday morning staff sales meeting. Attendance at it was considered mandatory. "Tad, you've just got to get up. I have got to leave in two minutes."

"But there's no rush. You know I don't have any classes until third period. But I'm getting up. I promised Desmond and Larry that I would meet them right after 8:00 at Murphy Park to practice our passing game."

"I still find it hard to believe that you don't have to be at school any earlier."

"Mom!", Tad interrupted her, now fully awake, "We've gone over this time and again! Those extra classes the last two years have paid off. I only lack the credits in four classes to graduate. And it just worked out this semester that I could get them all in a row beginning the third period. Same for Desmond and Larry." The snappish edge in Tad's voice settled back down as he added, "I really know what I'm doing Mom"

Kim came to his door and replied, "I know you do Tad. I've got to go. Let me give you a kiss." Before Tad could protest, she came into his room and gave him a peck on his forehead, the only part of his face still exposed after he had tried covering it up with his pillow to avoid the dreaded Mommy kiss. Then she was gone, "See you tonight after practice.", she called out as she went out the door to her car.

Now Tad waited in the outer office with the school secretary, Lou Ann Gordon for Mr. Rasco to get off the phone. Inside his office, Rasco was winding down a talk on the phone with an unhappy parent about how his son was being treated unfairly by his math teacher when homework was assigned. Or was it his daughter? Son? Daughter? Rasco no longer knew these days. He had spent 25 years in this office and frankly was needing to get away from it before the job got to him. He knew he wasn't as mentally sharp as he had been. And with high school students, you couldn't let that happen. At times he seemed to have spells of early dementia, mainly in saying things that on the surface were outrageous. For instance, he had reacted to a complaint from the janitors that kids were coming to school after hours to work on their projects out in the halls and undoing the janitors' cleanup jobs in the process. His response to that had been to make an announcement over the p.a. system the next morning that "Armed guards had been hired to patrol the halls at night with strict orders to shoot to kill. Students therefore should stay away from the halls of Honey Oaks High at night." Mrs. Gordon has managed to cover for him on that one as calls of incredulity and outrage poured in from the staff. She said he was just kidding. It was just a way to call attention to the need for the kids to respect the janitors' work and clean up their messes.

Mrs. Gordon saw the light go off her phone signaling her that Mr. Rasco was through with that parent. "You can go in now Tad." Tad stood up, his long lanky legs coming unwound from being stretched out on the floor in the outer office. He went through the door into Rasco's office. The principal was seated at his big oak desk. It was covered with knick knacks and gifts related to the Bumblebees that he had received through the years. A double-sized matching oak credenza was filled with more Honey Oaks memorabilia interspersed with books related to school administration. The wall opposite the door into the office was filled with plagues, certificates and pictures, all depicting special moments in Rasco's career.

He peered over his spectacles at Tad and said hello, "Why are you here in my office Whittaker? Are you in trouble in one of your classes?"

"No sir, I just wanted to talk to you about the murder."

"What about it? The sheriff still doesn't have anyone that might have done it."

"I know. But what if I saw something that might be related to the murder?"

"Are you saying you know something?", asked Rasco suddenly alert to what Tad was saying.

"I'm just saying that I saw a person around the Bee Hive shortly before Mr Slater was killed. I haven't said anything about it yet. Do you think I should tell Sheriff Gumby what I saw?"

"By all means Tad, if you know something, tell the sheriff! We need to get this solved. Honey Oaks and this school are in turmoil over this. You can't believe how many calls daily I get on it. Let me get Gumby on the phone and see when and where he can see you. If it's here, you can use the conference room. Mrs. Gordon, get Sheriff Gumby on the line for me!"

Dalton got the call from his dispatcher as he was driving to meet with a reporter for an interview about the very subject of lack of progress in solving the murder. The reporter was with the Dallas Morning News. His editor noted that the Bumblebees were coming to the Metroplex to play Friday and thought maybe there could be a tie in between the crime and the game. He pulled over to the shoulder of the highway and put his cruiser in idle as he dialed Honey Oaks High on his cell phone. "Mr Rasco, please. This is Dalton Gumby returning his call."

"Hello Sheriff, this is Leon Rasco. Thanks for calling back."

"What's on your mind Mr. Rasco?"

"I have Tad Whittaker in my office. He thinks he might have seen somebody or something at Barrett Bradwell before Justin Slater was killed. I told him you would like to talk to him as soon as possible. Can you come to the school now?"

"Mr. Rasco, I'm on my way to an appointment north of here. By the time I can get through and come back, it would be an hour or so. Could Tad meet me at my office then?"

Rasco turned towards Tad and said, "The sheriff would like to have you come to his office in an hour. Do you have any tests to take or papers to turn in today?"

"I have my English essay to turn in to Mrs. Laird in the fifth period, but that's all."

"Whittaker why don't you stop by her room and turn it in now? Then I can give you excused absences for how ever long it takes you over at Sheriff Gumby's." Tad nodded his acceptance and Rasco resumed talking to the sheriff, "Tad can do that. He'll be there in your office in an hour."

"That's great, I'm about two minutes away from the Brighton Diner where a reporter from Dallas is wanting to interview, no, make that harass me, about the murder since Honey Oaks is coming to Colleyville Southside Friday. I can cut his questions short saying I have a new lead in the case that just came to me. And I have to get right back to follow it up. I hope Tad really has something. It's been hard getting anything to break right on Justin's slaying."

"So do I Sheriff. We're ready to get this moving. Tad will be there in an hour."

CHAPTER XIII

Tad parked his pickup in the visitors section of the Feaster County Sheriff's Department parking lot. The late September morning was warm and sunny. But Tad was feeling chilled and scared as he walked to the entrance into the Sheriff's Department. He was wearing his Honey Oaks High letter jacket and pulled it tightly around him, declining to snap it closed. Inside he told the receptionist who he was and that he had an appointment with Sheriff Gumby. She had him take a seat while she phoned into Gumby's office. "He will be right with you.", she said. Tad thanked her and picked up a sports magazine which he nervously thumbed through.

He was startled by the booming voice of Gumby, "Tad! Thanks for coming. Let's go into my office to talk." Dalton held out his hand to shake Tad's hand.

Tad extended his right hand and said shyly, "Thanks Sheriff Gumby. I really feel weird even being here." Gumby ignored his comment as he continued to hold and shake Tad's hand.

He looked down at it and queried Tad, "Isn't this the hand that's destroying all the defenses Honey Oaks faced this year?"

Tad looked at him with a surprised look and said, "It certainly didn't destroy anything against Turnersborough." Gumby's face visibly reddened at the remark. He had heard many of the comments about his handling of the murder investigation that first 24 hours had hurt the Bumblebees more than the shock of Justin's slaying.

Dalton back-pedaled, "Sorry Tad, you can't blame yourself for Turnersborough. There was a lot going on that weekend which got everyone out of kilter."

"And that's why I'm here Sheriff. I saw somebody go into the Bee Hive before Mr. Slater was killed that I wish I hadn't seen."

Gumby sat up straight, his eyes wide-open as it sank in that maybe Tad had the lead he had been needing to get a break in the nine day old case. He took a legal pad out of the middle drawer on his desk and at the same time took a ball point pen from his shirt pocket. "Alright Tad.", he asked breathlessly, "Tell me about it." Tad began by telling him about going up into the press box after icing his arm. "Why were you up there Tad?"

"I just wanted to get a look at the game program and look over the roster for the Tornadoes."

"Is that when you saw someone go into the Bee Hive?"

"Actually I saw two people go in there."

Gumby's interest was totally focused on Tad. "Who were they Tad?"

"The first was Mr. Slater carrying in the moneybags, The second was Coach Donaldson about three minutes later."

"What happened then?"

"I don't know. I left to go to the house before I had to report back to the stadium at 5:00. I didn't see anyone else go in or leave the Bee Hive before I left."

"What time did all this happen Tad?"

"I went up to the press box about 3:00 p.m. I was gone in about 10 minutes."

Gumby pondered Tad's statements a moment, then said, "Tad, I'm going to have to question Coach Donaldson about him being there at that time."

Tad reacted in a state of panic, "Sheriff, you can't tell him that it was me that you talked to! He would be deeply hurt that I came to you!"

"Tad, you needed to come forward. Slater's killer needs to be found. Whether it's Coach Donaldson or someone else. Don't worry, I can talk to him without revealing that you came to me. Who knows Tad. Maybe he had a good reason to be there that's totally legit. As mad as he was at me for making the entire stadium a crime scene and causing the game to be moved, I can't imagine him killing Slater for any reason. I'll stay in touch, but I'm going to come to practice today and catch him to talk when it ends."

"Whew! Thanks Sheriff."

Gumby arrived at Barrett Bradwell Stadium at 5:30 and caught the last 30 minutes of practice. As it ended and most of the players headed to the locker room to shower and change, he came down out of the stands and stood on the track close to Coach Donaldson. He waited as Donaldson finished talking to a couple of players who had stayed late to update him on their classes they had been close to failing. They were now being tutored and the progress report they gave seemed to satisfy him. But he had already checked with their teachers and knew how they stood. He just wanted to hear it from them. The two headed for the locker room and Gumby stepped towards Donaldson. "Coach, I need to visit with you. Let's go sit in the stands where we can have some privacy."

Matt was taken back by the request, but replied, "Sure Sheriff, but what's this all about?"

Gumby waited until they had climbed up 10 rows and were isolated in an area above the 20 yard line. "As you know Coach, we haven't had anything to break yet on Justin's killing. But today I got a lead I'm following up."

"Oh really, what would that be?"

"Coach, I hope you have a good explanation, but somebody told me that he saw you go in the Bee Hive shortly after Justin went in, a little after three that Friday. Why did you go there at that time?" Donaldson's demeanor changed back to the way it had been a week ago yesterday morning when he was so furious at Gumby's actions. Then he thought that had played a part in the Bumble Bees losing to Turnersborough. Now he knew he was the one on the hot seat with potentially bigger consequences to him than losing a non-district football game.

Gumby noted how Donaldson puffed up again and got red in the face as he answered the question. The sheriff also noted the righteous indignation that flew out from Donaldson as he responded, "Yes I went there to see Slater, but just to make a request. Then I left and he was just fine as I went out the door. Who even said anything to you?", asked Donaldson in a voice loud enough to destroy any vestige of privacy Gumby had tried to have in going up into the stands.

Gumby persisted, "What kind of request?"

Donaldson came right back, "I was asking for the Booster Club to buy some medical supplies that we were low on and needed to replenish before very many more games went by. Slater said they could do it with no problem. I thanked him and I left!"

Gumby gave the big coach his stare-down look and asked the obvious queston, "Can you prove that?"

Donaldson looked dumbfounded briefly, but then the sequence of events from 13 days earlier came back to him. "Yes I can Sheriff! First of all after he agreed to the Booster Club spending the money, I picked up the phone in the Bee Hive and called on the extension to our trainer, Hank Carlisle. I told him to place the order. He said he would call it in then to catch the supplier, an East Coast company, before it closed for the weekend. Then I left the Bee Hive to keep getting ready for the game. Justin was just fine Gumby! So who told you I was even there?"

"It doesn't matter, Your story sounds plausible. Of course I will follow up with Carlisle and the supplier to verify what you said. If it's as you said, I'm still sucking hind teat in getting anywhere. Thanks for your time. Good luck at Southside Friday." Donaldson's eyes trailed Gumby as he walked up to the stadium concourse and headed for his cruiser.

"Thank God I have a story that can be easily verified.", reflected Donaldson. "Other wise, I might be sitting in jail Friday instead of coaching the Bumble Bees in the Metroplex."

CHAPTER XIV

Late that afternoon, Clayfour worked at his desk at the gin and noted by glancing at the antique railroad clock hanging on the wall opposite him that it was nearly 6:00. There were two windows on that wall on either side of the clock that looked out at the receiving dock in the gin yard. Soon the college students who worked part time for him would be leaving for the day. He asked Diana to have Tommy Randall, a sophomore at Tarleton and a three year part-time employee of the gin come see him before clocking out. Tommy soon came to Clayfour's office. He was a six-footer with red hair, freckles and an infectious grin. "You wanted to see me Mr. Peterson?"

"Yes Tommy, don't you have a MWF afternoon class with Hootie?"

"Dr. McGuire? Oh sure, ag-eco from 3:00 to 4:00 those days."

"Is it true that he gives you a lot of walks on Fridays?"

Tommy thought about it a second or two, then responded, "As a matter of fact he does Mr. Peterson. How did you know that?"

"Let's just say Tommy, that yours is not the first class that he's ever given walks. What I want to see is if you'd like to earn some extra money the next Friday he gives your class a walk."

"Well I think so Mr. Peterson. What would I have to do?"

Clayfour responded, "Well first of all Tommy, you can just call me Clayfour instead of Mr. Peterson. After all this is the third fall semester that you've worked here at the gin. It's okay if you lighten up on the formalities."

"Well thanks Mr. Pete, uh Clayfour. But what kind of work would I do?"

"Tommy it's pretty simple, but one you will have to keep to yourself and not tell anyone what you're doing. But I will pay you an extra $5.00 an hour over what you make here plus any gas and meal expenses you would have on that Friday."

"All right!, Mr.Pete,uh Clayfour, that sounds great! So what will I be doing for you?"

Clayfour had swiveled his chair around to gaze at the other part-timers who were working by the receiving dock to shut down the equipment for the night. He spun back to look Tommy straight on. "Tommy, if Hootie or Dr. McGuire gives you that walk on Friday, I want you to find out where he goes and what he does after he lets the class out. But without him knowing what you're doing. It might be this Friday that he gives a walk. Can you do that okay?"

"I had wanted to go to the Honey Oaks game in Colleyville, but I don't have to, especially if this is important enough to you to pay me that extra money. Why do you want me to follow him anyway Clayfour?"

"I'm just interested personally for a friend of mine what he does do on those days. Hootie has always been a big Honey Oaks fan who likes to go to the games both in and out of town. So you could end up at the game anyway if that is where he goes. Anyway though, I would want you to follow him and note who he's with and where he goes on that Friday even if it's not to the game. Keep it to yourself of course, but contact me Saturday morning to tell me what you found out."

"What if he sees me following him?"

"Tommy, Tommy that shouldn't be a big deal. Probably you'll be in places where it's kind of natural for both of you to be there and bump into each other. Just act natural like you're about your business if you have to say anything to him."Clayfour added, "If he leaves campus and drives away, do you know what kind of car or pickup he drives?"

"No I don't Mr. Pete, er Clayfour."

"The school has reserved parking near the buildings where each faculty member teaches. Last time I was there, I remember walking by the spaces and seeing each prof's name printed on the little concrete barrier that is reserved for him or her. Why don't you check that out tomorrow when you're by the Agri-Business building?"

"Yeah, I'll do that just in case I have to follow him out of town or something."

Clayfour stood up to indicate that he was done. Tommy popped right up after him. Clayfour extended his hand and said, "Thanks Randall, I know I can count on you. Remember this is all hush-hush. Keep it to yourself. Keep all your receipts for gas and food and even the football ticket if you end up following him to the game. I'll pay you for those too. Make good notes about the people he sees, the time he spends in each location, addresses and anything else you think is worth knowing about." Tommy's infectious grin which displayed a small gap between his two upper front teeth came back to his face.

He took Clayfour's right hand in his right hand and shook it vigorously. "You bet I will Clayfour. This sounds exciting! Kind of cloak and dagger. Maybe I'll become a detective if I do this okay. Thanks for the opportunity. I won't let you down. See you tomorrow after I get out of school." Tommy headed for his car as soon as he left Clayfour's office reveling in the possibilities that this assignment could bring him.

Clayfour watched him pull out of the parking lot and said to himself, "I believe that Tommy will get the goods on Hootie just fine, if there are any to get."

CHAPTER XV

It was 8:15 Wednesday morning when Clayfour walked into the gin offices. Diana greeted him with, "About time. Sheriff Gumby's called here twice in the last 15 minutes trying to reach you. He said he couldn't get through to your cell phone."

"Yeah, I had it turned off driving in."

Diana had fixed him a cup of coffee and handed it to him now. "He sounds like he's got a burr under his saddle that can only be relieved by talking to you. Call him right now."

"Okay Diana, thanks for the java." He went into his office, plopped down in his chair and dialed Dalton. When he came on the line, Clayfour asked, "What's happening Dalton?"

"I had a call from the District Clerk's office this morning right at 8:00. Justin's will got filed. Jody in the Clerk's office tells me that his ex, Phyllis is squawking about what's in it."

"Oh really, why is that?"

"Apparently she thought that the will still had her in it. At least, the copy that she had listed her as an heir. But Justin made a new one after their divorce which cuts her out totally. She didn't know about it until Justin's lawyer filed it yester-day."

Clayfour remembered some of the ugly scenes between Justin and Phyllis which had spilled out of the closed doors in his office at Thompson Brothers. He noticed the tension between them at social gatherings that he, his wife Katherine and the Slaters had jointly attended. In moments when Phyllis thought she and

Justin were alone, she threatened and berated him without ceasing. But Clayfour had been back in the shadows on more than one of those occasions. He knew how venomous Phyllis could be. He felt relief for Justin when he finally moved out and filed for divorce. If ever two people needed to be apart, it was Justin and Phyllis.

Clayfour came back with the obvious, "Why would she even think that Justin would keep her in his will? All their kids are out of school so no obligations are there. She got half his assets when the divorce was settled. Boy, she must be greedy to think she's due more by still being in his will."

Gumby could stand it no longer, "Clayfour, think! If she's making all this noise about still being in the will, that elevates her as a suspect to me. Bumping him off to get the money she thought she had coming when he died!"

Clayfour said, "You're absolutely right Dalton. This bears looking into. I have had her in the back of my mind since the day of the funeral. I just hadn't gotten to checking her out as yet. I think I'll make a trip to the Clerk's office and see what that will says. After I make a couple of calls to follow up some other leads that are hanging."

Gumby said, "Oh yeah, that reminds me. I was told by Tad Whittaker that he had seen Coach Donaldson go into the Bee Hive just a few minutes after Justin got there. That's between you and me. Anyway, I talked to Donaldson about it and he said he had gone there to have the Booster Club get the team some extra medical supplies. He said the trainer could verify that and he had actually ordered the supplies that Friday immediately before the supplier on the East Coast shut down for the day being they are an hour ahead of us there. I checked with the trainer and the supplier and they verify his story."

Clayfour responded, "I am calling my friends at the regional cotton producers office in Lubbock to make sure T.L. Morgan really attended that seminar in Lubbock when Justin was killed. I'll let you know if that's not the case, but I think it will be true and take him off my list. As for Hootie, I have hired one of my student helpers who has a Friday afternoon class with him to hang around and see where he goes if he gives that class a walk. His reaction at Thompson Brothers the other day indicated to me that he did so that Friday Justin died and was trying to hide it when I asked him point-blank. I am supposed to get a report Saturday morning about what he does if he gives a Friday walk."

Gumby said, "I'm having the district clerk send me over a copy of the will this morning. After we both have looked at it, we can figure where to go next."

"One thing I have in mind is to pay a social call on Phyllis since we used to be close as a couple and see if I can learn anything just being around her. I' ll talk to you later."

The District Clerk's office was located conveniently on the first floor of the Feaster County Courthouse. Clayfour strolled in and was greeted by Jody, "Hey Clayfour, I bet I know why you're here. I already got a copy ready for you since Gumby told me that you would be here soon." She lifted a folder off the counter top that separated her from the general public and handed it to Clayfour with a big smile on her face. "Wait til you see what Justin's done, It's going to be the talk of the town. And for comparison purposes, I made you a copy of the old will so you can see the difference between them." Clayfour beamed his appreciation at Jody as he took both folders from her and retreated to a table to sit down and read them. He pulled out the old will to see what it said first. The only mention of Phyllis being in it was for a bequest of the balance remaining in his Thompson Brothers retirement fund, about $200,000.00 based on the actuarial projections that were shown in an accompanying folder from Thompson Brothers' Human Relations Department.

When Clayfour was satisfied with what Phyllis had coming in the old will, he turned his attention to the new will to see where the retirement fund money was now going. He raised his eyes in amazement when he got to that part of the will. Justin had redirected that money to be split 50-50 between his two alma maters, Texas A & M University and Honey Oaks High School. At A & M, it would go to the Business School to finance the purchase of programs related to the stock market that would help future Aggies be better prepared for a career as a stockbroker like him. The stipend for Honey Oaks High named the Booster Club to be its recipient and fund four $1,000.00 scholarships annually. The club could decide whether to fund the same student athlete for four years or just for the first year to get him or her started in college. Based on the grumbling he had heard at the Booster Club meeting Monday about Dalton's method of shutting down Barrett Bradwell as a crime scene and causing that expected revenue from the Turnersborough game to disappear, he knew that word of this bequest would make everyone at Honey Oaks High happier. The happiest group would be the senior parents who thought that their children were going to be denied Booster Club scholarships. He could see it being a big topic of conversation on the visitors side of Colleyville Southside Friday night. It might be worth going to the game just for that aspect of it.

Meantime he decided that seeing Phyllis as soon as possible might be in order. If her usual routine of the past 15 years was still being done, she would be working as a volunteer at the Ingleside Retirement Home reading to its residents on a one by one basis. Clayfour having observed her behavior with Justin so much couldn't imagine her being nice or helping out anyone at all. He had her pegged just right. It was a facade that she put on, endured actually from 10:00 to noon Wednesdays to give her public image an uplift. Katherine had volunteered with her for the past few years and that was how Clayfour knew her schedule. He figured it wouldn't bother her too much if he pulled her away from a resident that she was reading to for her reaction to Justin's new bequest.

At North Madison and Beech, where the Ingleside Retirement Home was located, Clayfour parked in its visitors section at 10:15 and slipped in the door. He walked down its halls listening for Phyllis's voice to be coming from a room where she would be reading poetry to a resident. He didn't have to go past too many doors before she could be heard in her loud voice impatiently reciting a Longfellow piece to a resident who was bed-ridden. He stopped at the door and listened for a moment before knocking. Phyllis came quickly and opened the door relieved to be able to stop reading for whatever the reason. "Clayfour, what are you doing here?"

"Hello Phyllis, I thought maybe Katherine was here today and was looking for her when I heard your voice."

"So why would you stop and talk to me if you're looking for Katherine?", asked Phyllis very leerily.

"Well, I heard the news from the courthouse that Justin had left money in his will to his two schools. I was just wondering if you knew that and felt good about his doing so?" Her face reddened in an explosion of anger when she answered. Her voice was lowered to a level designed to get her message across, but let him know that she wasn't happy about the change in the will.

"Clayfour, I can't believe you think that would please me to have money ripped from me by that bastard in one final act to deprive me of what I was entitled to."

"Phyllis, I've known the two of you ever since you married and Justin for many years before that. I know that your marriage wasn't the greatest, but didn't you get half of his assets when you divorced in a fair split of what had built up between you two while you were married?"

"Well, yes."

"And with your kids all gone and him providing for them in the will anyway, weren't they taken care of adequately?"

"I guess so.", stammered Phyllis.

"So why would you want his retirement fund also instead of seeing him help other students to further their education by giving it to the two schools?"

"Because I had plans for that money to build on to the house a new recreational wing. Now I can't and frankly it's made me mad."

"Phyllis, you know whoever killed Justin hasn't been found. Would it have been possible that you were thinking about doing him in thinking that money would be there for you if he were gone?"

Phyllis completely lost it when Clayfour asked that question. "No! Of course not! My kids had a good relationship with their father which I wanted to continue for their sakes! I may have wanted that money, but all in good time. How can you even think that I would have anything to do with it?"

Clayfour noticed several aides coming down the hall drawn by the explosion from Phyllis. "Frankly, I can't imagine it Phyllis, despite witnessing the battles between the two of you at times that I didn't want to. It wasn't good for you two for so long, but I can't see you going so far as to kill him or have him killed. But from being in police work in Dallas for all those years, I can tell you that Sheriff Gumby is considering all possible suspects especially since he has yet to arrest anybody. Phyllis, I hope that you have a good alibi for that day. And I suggest that your bellyaching about the change in the will that I hear you're doing all over town is putting the light on you as someone for Gumby to check out."

Clayfour stepped out of the room just as the staff arrived and said, "I better get to going Phyllis. You have an audience waiting to hear the rest of Longfellow."

As he strode away from the room, he heard the sound of the poetry book being thrown down the hall toward him with a cry from her, "You're a bastard too!" The book landed harmlessly near his feet as he walked on out of the Ingleside Retirement Home thinking Dalton would still have some work to do on this one.

CHAPTER XVI

"I might as well jump from the frying pan into the fire.", thought Clayfour as he pulled back onto Beech Street from the Ingleside Retirement Home parking lot. His thoughts continued, "It can't get any worse with Freddy Benjamin than it just was with Phyliss. I think I'll go see him now." Benjamin was the stock and commodity broker Justin had fired five years earlier after numerous clients had complained about the way he handled their accounts. He would take their orders, but fail to enter them timely, using discretion that they hadn't granted him to place their orders after a market move that they were trying to avoid had already begun. In some of those cases, his family members who had accounts with him had positions in the same securities or commodities that were opposite those of the clients who ended up being the losers on those trades. He was taking care of his own whose relationship to him had not been disclosed on the new account forms to Justin in the Honey Oaks office and to Thompson Brothers in the Atlanta home office.

But that wasn't all. Despite his swift calculating mind, Benjamin also had the habit of just forgetting to turn in orders particularly if the clients did hint at him using his discretion to help them out. Most commonly, one of them had said to him, "If you see the market start to drop on my position, just sell it out. You don't have to call me or anything. Just take care of me." Inevitably that would lead to him finally remembering those instructions when it was too late to help the client cut his or her losses. He wasn't supposed to have done that in the first place since discretion was a big no-no in the brokerage industry. It was only allowed under the strictest of circumstances and had to be well supported by documentation signed by both parties. His bad recollection of hearing his clients even saying anything until after their losses had started running made them lose lots of money, no thanks to him.Benjamin would liquidate their positions too late and call back the results to them giving excuses such as, "There were too many orders ahead of you." or "Justin had us in a meeting in his office when the down slide started and I couldn't get to it." His excuses were clever and crafty, but to those clients who noted his evasiveness and shiftiness of his eyes when he told them in person what had happened to their accounts, they seemed too contrived.

In the meantime, Justin had learned of the undisclosed family ties between Freddy and a number of his accounts. He noted how well those accounts had prospered in making high-risk trades that normally caused clients to lose money. Some of the clients on the other sides of those trades had begun complaining to him that Benjamin wasn't handling their accounts properly. A definite conflict of interest existed. When the complaints started coming in about their orders not being carried out, Justin had had enough. He previously had warned Freddy to keep his nose clean.

When he called the young broker into office to discuss the situation, Freddy went berserk. He denied the complaints on all counts and called Justin a lot of names that went too far. Both men were red in the face and stood toe to toe glaring at each other. The sweaters in the bullpen and the other brokers stood silently outside Justin's office listening to the vocal explosions inside. Though Freddy was a foot shorter than Justin, he managed to stay in Justin's face becoming more and more violent. Finally Justin could take no more, "Freddy, you're done here! I want you gone by the time the market closes!", yelled Justin into the little man's face. That shut Freddy up and he stalked out of the office back to his desk. All the while he was throwing looks of hatred back at Justin.

It took Freddy several hours to call his clients that were his family members, explain what was happening and to pack up his desk. Justin watched his progress from his desk as he called the compliance department of Thompson Brothers at the home office in Atlanta to tell its officers what had just happened in the Honey Oaks office. After briefing them and receiving instructions of how to proceed, Justin went out to Freddy's desk. Freddy looked up at him and snapped, "What now?"

"Just calm down Freddy. I talked to compliance and advised them you're leaving. I want you to know we will help you transfer clients if that's what they want and not divide them up like other brokers do. Also, if any of them want to make a trade before you get them transferred, I'll handle those trades, but continue to credit you with the commissions until the end of the production month. We won't officially terminate your license until then. That should give you a chance to hang your ticket somewhere." Still grumbling, Freddy barely acknowledged Justin's gesture, but did mumble a thanks before leaving Thompson Brothers for good.

He moved to a smaller brokerage firm, Gilbert and Company., Inc which focused on commodities. With word out about him after the flareup in the office, about the only accounts that moved with him were the ones in his family. But he had negotiated a bigger payout on his production from his new employer. The percentage increase easily offset the lost income from the accounts that stayed at Thompson Brothers. Then his being on the right side of a series of market moves in different commodities over the next two years had brought him more clients than before. The fact that it was luck and had nothing to do with Freddy's ability to see the trends developing and read the markets (In reality he was dumber than dirt in knowing what was going on in the world that caused markets to act the way that they did) didn't matter at all. Soon he was thriving more than before. While he stopped bad mouthing Justin Slater and Thompson Brothers on a daily basis, he still expressed his resentment every once in a while. At least that was the way Clayfour was hearing it. The last minute show of generosity by Justin in keeping him licensed there while he moved to Gilbert & Company was not forgotten by Freddy. He also was thankful that Justin didn't follow the old brokerage house custom of dividing up a broker's accounts among the remaining brokers as soon as the market closed on the afternoon he or she had died, retired, changed firms or been fired. The idea put forth by the branch managers in doing so was for the best interests of the clients. But to the brokers dividing up the accounts, it was more like Christmas in July gaining access to accounts previously off limits to them. And most of them that they gained they would retain.

Gilbert & Company. Inc. was located on Fannin Street three blocks northwest of the Feaster County Courthouse. Its clients had to park on the streets and walk into the office from the sidewalk in front of the building. It took the south third of the building. Fishburne's Fine Clothiers took the other two thirds of the store front. Clayfour found a vacant parking space a block down the street. He walked back up to Gilbert & Company and went into the office. In a continuous manner, the stock and commodity boards were flashing trade after trade. There were a half dozen chairs for the customers, three of which were occupied.

It was on only one occasion four years earlier that Clayfour had been in this office. Now he was searching the three private offices behind the customer chairs for Freddy's office. Each of those offices had big glass walls that gave the broker and his clients a view of the boards sending across the transactions in regular and rapid sequence. The third office away from the entrance turned out to belong to Freddy. Clayfour saw the little man on the phone. He noted again as he had at the funeral that his hair was thinning out drastically. Benjamin wore glasses that Clayfour swore were thicker than the last pair he had seen him wearing. He glanced up from his phone and quote machine, saw Clayfour and waved him to come in.

"Hello Clayfour, what brings you here? I thought you always hung out at Thompson Brothers."

"Yes that's usually true, but I have a couple of my ginning customers that I think need to be hedging their crops. I haven't seen or heard of them doing so at Thompson Brothers. Maybe you would know since the bank's financing them and wants its risk minimized. Apparently they're cutting it close on making a profit or losing."

"Who are you talking about Clayfour?"

"Joseph Burleson and Larry Forsyth."

"No, I don't have either of them on the books."

"I'm sure their banker is going to insist on them putting on a hedge any day now. Maybe you'll get their business."

"Well, thanks for stopping by."

"Yeah I was driving by and thought of that. I knew I hadn't seen you since the funeral and decided to drop in and say hello."

"You were a pallbearer there. I noticed you when I walked by Justin's casket."

"In a way I was surprised to see you paying your respects since I recall him firing you."

"Well yes he did and I was pretty angry when it happened. But since then, the more I've thought about it, the more I decided that I deserved it Then when a lot of my clients wouldn't move their accounts here, I did a lot of soul-searching and came to the realization that I hadn't treated them right. When they complained to Justin, he had to take action. At first I felt it was me being wronged. That's when I was publicly blasting Justin and Thompson even months after I landed here at Gilbert. But the more I realized I had lost a lot of customers, the more it dawned on me it was my actions causing that. Had I been handling my business ethically and properly, it wouldn't have happened. Bottom line Clayfour, I took responsibility for my actions and forgave Justin though he had done nothing wrong to be forgiven for." Freddy paused for a moment while Clayfour sat silently on the other side of the desk waiting for him to finish

But he did ask, "It now sounds like you're putting your clients first, even those not your family members?"

"You're exactly right. It really has turned my life around. Now I have a growing clientele because the ones I have keep bringing others to me because of the attention I'm giving their accounts. Everyone is happy with the way I handle their accounts and needs."

By now Clayfour was feeling strongly Freddy couldn't be considered a prime suspect. Then Freddy jumped up and said, "Let me show you something that came from Justin canning me that I am very proud of."He stepped back to a section of wall behind his desk where various plaques and certificates were hung and took one of them off the wall. Beaming with pride he carried it to Clayfour and handed it to him. He said, "I got this simply because Justin fired me. I learned how to be a better person and broker because of it. This plaque backs up that statement. Gilbert & Co. awarded it to me this month at their annual awards banquet in Chicago." Clayfour read the plaque with interest, "This is awarded to Freddy Benjamin for having the highest client satisfaction rating of all the brokers associated with Gilbert & Co., Inc." The September 10th date on it jumped out at Clayfour like a beacon flashing in the water.

Freddy took back the plaque and stated, "Isn't it ironic? The day I was in Chicago receiving this award was the Friday that Justin got killed. I had planned to show it to him the next Monday and thank him for what he did for me. Of course, I didn't get the chance. But I did pay him my final respects at the funeral. He was quite a man as the turnout for his service showed."

"Wow Freddy!", exclaimed Clayfour, "Justin really did make a difference in your life though it was a hard lesson to learn. Congratulations on this achievement. You probably realize why I was so honored to be a pallbearer at the service of a man who's been my best friend since grade school." Clayfour reached out and took Freddy's hand in a firm clasp. As he vigorously shook it, he looked him in the eye and said, "I've got to run, but it's been good seeing you. I'm going to encourage Burleson and Forsyth to come put on their hedges with you." Freddy smiled as Clayfour headed for the front door turning to wave goodby before he exited Gilbert & Co. Outside his thoughts were to scratch Freddy off his suspect list and move on to Dick Nichols. Right now he would head back to Peterson Gin for a while before heading to Nichols' office right as the lunch hour ended.

CHAPTER XVII

When he got back to his truck, he called his office. Diana answered, "Peterson Gin Co"

."Hey Diana, anything shaking there?"

"No Clayfour, it's pretty quiet."

"I am going to come in for an hour or so. But first I'm stopping at Texas Burger to get a cheeseburger. Do you want me to pick something up for you?"

"No, if you're going to be here during the lunch hour, I think I'll get out and buy me a new sweater before it turns cold."

"Diana that will be fine. I need to go out about 12:50. Can you make it back by then?"

"Oh sure Clayfour, I'm going to the mall so it won't take me too long to get back to the office." "Great Diana. Do me a favor and call Texas Burger. Order me a cheeseburger with both mayonnaise and mustard. Cut the pickles. I'll be at the drive through window in seven or eight minutes. I should be there in the office in about 15 minutes."

"Okay Boss,you got it. You can give me my tip when you get here."

"The only tip I'll have for you is don't be such a wise ass.! I pay you plenty so I'm not going to pay tips on top of that."

"Clayfour you can't blame a girl for trying can you?" The laughter in Diana's voice came through the phone. Just two business associates and close friends who enjoyed being together in a highly successful business relationship.

Clayfour was back to the office in just 12 minutes, the sack in his hand giving off a good smell of grilled burger. Diana had him a diet root beer waiting which she handed to him as they met at the front door. "You have two phone calls to return. The numbers are on your desk."

"Okay, thanks. I'll see you in an hour. Happy shopping." He sat at his desk slowly chewing his burger, looked at the two calls and decided that they could wait. Right now he wanted to bone up on Dick Nichols and what happened between him and Justin that raised his hackles the day he saw him at the funeral.

It finally clicked that Justin had sued Nichols but he couldn't remember the details. He called the courthouse and asked the district clerk's office to dig them up and fax it to him very quickly. He was highly respected in that office and its staff would do almost anything to accommodate him. The fax came to him in about 15 minutes. Clayfour scanned the original petition. Nichols got sued because he hadn't paid for an new stock issue or IPO after Justin had gotten him all the stock he had asked for. When the issue had tanked instead of jumping dramatically in price as was the case in so many other IPO's, Nichols saw a big loss facing him and denied giving Justin the order. Justin took immediate action and cut the losses by selling the 5000 share position into a falling market. The loss was $20,400.00. Justin going on his past business relationship with Dick in giving him new issues thought he would honor his order and make good on his loss. But Nichols stayed adamant that he hadn't given Justin the order. So it ended up in district court.

It wasn't too hard for Justin to make his case. He produced records of Dick's trades showing how he had regularly purchased IPO's in addition to trading heavily in other securities. Nichols saw the potential of IPO's in a hot market. A company like Electronic Data Systems, Microsoft or Golden State Foods would file to make its first ever public stock offering and demand for the shares would go through the roof. Justin's regular clients would give him orders for 10,00 shares if he could get them into the offering. What they didn't realize was that Thompson Brothers had to be invited into the syndicate of brokerage firms making the offering. Because it wasn't a large firm or possessed a special cachet in corporate finance, Thompson Brothers usually came into an offering as a second tier firm getting a minimal number of shares to distribute to its clients who put in an indication of interest to purchase them. Collectively all of Thompson Brothers' clients who said that they were willing to buy 100,000 shares might get only 2,000 shares to spread among the 33 offices of the firm. That meant an office might get only 50 to 100 shares of the latest hot issue to give to its clients. Those clients lucky enough to receive them sometimes saw gains of 50% or more in the first hour or so after they began to trade.

Nichols figured out that if he always put in an indication of interest on every new issue and supplemented it by being an aggressive trader in other stocks and options, he would gain favor from Justin in getting the really hot new IPO's. Most clients were not aware of how potent the IPO market could be for their accounts and rarely asked Justin for them. Nichols had a three year history of buying IPO's and always paying for them. He had made over $50,000.00 in profits over that time selling the IPO's as soon as the trading syndicates for each issue dissolved.

The testimony in the trial by Justin accompanied by a paper trail of indications of interest put in by Dick gave conclusive evidence that he regularly said he would take anywhere from 10,000 shares on up. Of course he knew that he would be lucky to get 100 shares, let alone an occasional 200 share bonanza. So he put in the orders with no qualms that he would ever have to pay what he had asked for. When he got 5,000 shares of Touchstone Chemical at $20.00 a share and it promptly dropped to $18.00 a share the first day of trading, he was shocked and unprepared to pay for it. Justin gave him until the end of the three business day settlement period to make good on the trade. By then it was down to $16.00 a share when Justin sold out the position.

The jury hearing the evidence in the trial weighed it realizing it overwhelmingly favored Justin and awarded him and Thompson Brothers the money to cover the loss and attorney's fees. Nichols filed for bankruptcy though Justin couldn't believe he even needed to based on all the documented profits he had previously made as Justin's client. The loss embittered Justin toward Nichols as he had to take half of it. Had Dick been a new client putting in those orders, Thompson Brothers would have charged the whole loss to him. But Nichols' three year track record of always paying for his trades before saved Slater from the full $20,000.00 plus loss. Still Justin called every broker around to warn them not to accept orders from Nichols unless he paid for the trades upfront with good funds. Justin's actions and his being forced into bankruptcy made Dick very bitter in turn toward his former broker. After perusing the law suit information for an half hour or so while he slowly ate his burger, Clayfour heard the front door open signaling that Diana had returned. He washed and dried his hands and told

Diana he would be out of the office for an hour or so. He was on his way to Dick Nichols' office.

Nichols ran a real estate mortgage and property management business which was located at the corner of Washington Avenue and Cedar Street. It was about two miles northeast of Peterson Gin. When Clayfour turned onto Washington at Pecan Street, he was four blocks from Dick's office. Then he noticed the flashing lights of several police cars and other emergency vehicles around Nichols' office. He sped up to get there. As he got closer, he could see a mobil crime scene lab truck from the Texas Department of Public Safety, an ambulance with its lights off, the pickup of Justice of the Peace #2 Theodore Pullman, three Honey Oaks police cars and two Feaster County Sheriff's Department cars including Dalton Gumby's cruiser. There was a crime scene tape around the premises of Nichols Mortgage and Property Management Services. Two Honey Oaks police officers and a Feaster County deputy stood guard at various points of the tape.

Gumby had just stepped out of the office when he saw Clayfour approaching. He yelled, "Hey Clayfour come here!" To one of the policeman at the tape and closest to Clayfour, he gestured, "It's okay. Let him in."

Clayfour met Dalton at the front door as he was about to reenter the building. "What's going on Dalton? Who's dead?", asked Clayfour pretty sure he already knew the answers.

"It's Dick Nichols. Looks like he made some enemies along the way.", replied Dalton. "Come in and see for yourself."

"That's strange. I was on my way here to see him anyway. He was one of those I saw at the funeral who could have had reason to kill Justin."

"What happened?", asked Dalton.

"In the short version, he didn't pay for some stock that he had clearly ordered. The stock went down. Justin sold it for a $20,000.00 loss and he and Thompson Brothers sued Dick. He took bankruptcy when the verdict went against him. Justin let every broker in town know what happened so Nichols couldn't sting them. That's why he might have wanted to kill Justin."

Dalton led Clayfour into Nichols' private office. There slumped in his leather chair with his head thrown back against the pillow rest was Nichols. There appeared to be three wounds in his chest and right shoulder from bullets fired from a gun at him at close range. His right hand which lay in his lap also had a bullet hole in it as if he had thrown his hand up at the last moment to ward off the shots. Clayfour asked Dalton, "When do you think this happened?"

"We got a 911 call about 12:25 p.m. It came from someone in the next office. She heard the shots and hid under a desk pulling the phone down with her."

"Did she say she saw anybody?"

"No, she stayed under the desk after she called us until she heard the sirens and then us and the cops rushing in here."

"How long did it take to get here after her call?"

"Clayfour I noted that I arrived here at 12:30 p.m. The other police vehicles were arriving about the same time. When we saw the body, we called for the DPS Mobile Crime Lab. They just happened to be in town for a meeting with the local forensics officers. They got here 15 minutes ago."

Two of the DPS officers from the mobile lab were trying to dust the desk and other nearby furniture for fingerprints. They asked Clayfour and Dalton to step back out of their way. That was a signal to Peterson and Gumby to step out of the room. Clayfour commented, "Since he's dead, I don't see much point at this stage of trying to investigate him now. I am still checking on Hootie. I will get information on what he does in Stephenville on Friday afternoons when he gives his last class a walk fairly early Saturday morning. Then there's Phyllis Slater. She threw a fit and a book at me this morning when I brought this matter up of her bitching and moaning about Justin changing the will raising your suspicions about her. She didn't like what I said. That needs to be followed up."

"I'll get on it immediately.", replied Dalton.

"Oh one other person I saw today was Freddy Benjamin. Do you remember him and the time Justin fired him?"

"Wasn't that five or six years ago?"

"It was five years ago. There were a lot of hard feelings and a lot of comments by Freddy afterwards. But the reasons for Justin firing him seemed to have gone away. He's apparently so respected by his clients now that Gilbert & Co. gave him the award for having the highest client satisfaction of any broker nationwide in his company. And get this Dalton. he was given the award in Chicago the day Justin was killed. He has a plaque which Gilbert & Co. gave him then which has that date on it. He was a long ways from Honey Oaks that day."

Gumby retorted, "That doesn't mean that he couldn't have paid someone to do it for him. That's pretty convenient Clayfour."

Clayfour nodded in agreement, "I know what you mean Dalton. However he had a whole lot to say about how being fired and losing a number of his clients was a wakeup call for him. He had forgiven Justin and had planned to see him Monday to show off that plaque and thank him for making him change by the action of firing him. Dalton I'm not totally good at reading human nature, but I do a pretty fair job of it. I would say that he's sincere and we can rule him out as a suspect."

"Well, tht's just great Clayfour, but we're almost back to square one. Only Hootie and Phyllis Slater are still possible suspects in your evaluations. And they'll probably have something that clears them pretty quick. Meantime the media and the public continue to clamor for me to get something done that will put this crime to rest."

Clayfour gave Dalton a look of sympathy and understanding before replying, "I know it's tough now. But both of us are doing the best we can. Something will break soon. I just feel it in my bones."

Dalton shot back, "Tomorrow will be two weeks since the killing. I sure hope so. What do you have planned tomorrow anyway?"

"I still think that we're missing something from Honey Oaks High that could help us. I'm using that as an excuse to go to Colleyville Southside for the game tomorrow night. Sitting in the crowd might give me something, though what it would be, I don't know."

"Okay, you do that. I'll contact Phyllis and question her in more detail in the morning."

"Good luck Dalton, she's hell on wheels. She could give you fits."

"Clayfour, I'm ahead of her. She'll probably be surprised when I make contact in the morning. I'll talk to you no later than Saturday afternoon. Plan on meeting around noon at Danny's Ribs to exchange info."

Clayfour groaned at the thought of the last meal that he had eaten there. "Okay Dalton, but I'm only having a smoked turkey sandwich this time. Just to give you fair warning." Dalton turned his attention back on the murder scene in Dick Nichols' office. Clayfour went back under the crime scene tape and headed back to his office for the rest of the afternoon.

CHAPTER XVIII

Dalton's assumption that he was going to surprise Phyllis went completely out the window Friday morning. At 8:05 she and her attorney Lucy Morehouse stomped noisily into his office demanding of his secretary Linda they wanted to see him right now. Morehouse had represented Phyllis in her divorce from Justin. That was her special niche in the legal profession, to represent wealthy women in divorces and go for the jugular in getting settlements out of their soon to be exes. Her clients had done well by her representation. She and Phyllis both were reeking of Geoffrey Beene, Guicci, Cartier, Halston and Versace as they exploded into the sheriff's office. Gumby had just arrived at the Feaster County Law Enforcement Center only five minutes earlier. He correctly assumed that the two women must have been lying in wait for him to pull his cruiser into the designated parking spot on the lot for him. Now they were barking at Linda in the outer office to let them go in and see Dalton. Linda was flustered by their shrill verbal demands, but tried to gain some semblance of control and decorum by asking, "Do you have an appointment with the sheriff? I don't show it on my calendar."

Inside his office Dalton momentarily buried his head in his hands as he heard Morehouse fire right back, "Hell no Ms. Owens! We don't need an appointment. We just need to see him now. We have plenty to say to him."

Rather than subject Linda to anymore of their rudeness, Dalton went to the door, opened it and said, "You can quit harassing Linda with your abusive style Lucy. Come in and tell me what's so important that you two come storming in here in a rage."

"You bet we'll let you know Gumby!" Both women were almost frothing at the mouth they were so agitated. They stomped inside and stood on the other side of his desk. Dalton walked around to his chair and motioned them to have a seat. Lucy continued to stand and glared at the sheriff. Finally she spoke, "Phyllis said Clayfour confronted her at the retirement home yesterday about her being upset with the change in Justin's will. He said it was probably raising your suspicions that maybe she had something to do with Justin's death thinking that she was still in the will. His comments upset her and some of the residents at Ingleside. She couldn't continue reading the poetry to them which they love to hear so much from Phyllis. It's almost like he was trespassing to be there. And what does he have to do with the investigation anyway.?"

Dalton tried again asking them to take a seat as he sat down in his chair. When they continued to stand, he directed his attention at Phyllis, "Phyllis, Clayfour and Justin were best friends since Honey Oaks Elementary. You well know that. You also know his wife Katherine volunteers at Ingleside the same as you. He was within his rights to go looking for her there since that's the time she volunteers at Ingleside. He told me it was all over the courthouse about your blowing up when the new will was filed with the district clerk. Maybe he was trying to do you a favor as a long-time friend to tell you to cool it. Because what he said is very true. Your actions and your greediness stand out especially when there's been no one arrested in two weeks for Justin's killing. Even if your marriage was a disaster, you're still the mother of his children. I would think that for their sakes and those of your grandchildren, you would want this crime settled as soon as possible. Besides I understand you got half of what Justin had earned and accumulated in the divorce settlement. Wasn't that enough for you anyway? And where were you two weeks ago today?"

Phyllis shrunk somewhat at his rebuttal which put her on the defensive, but not for long. She started in on Dalton, "Of course I know my children and grandchildren are devastated by this. They do want the killer found. But it's not me and I am not greedy. Justin had that money earmarked for me in the will. I never dreamed that he would change it for others outside the family to have."

"The only one in the family that would have received it was you Phyllis, not Julie, Charles or Alton. They were well taken care of otherwise in his will. And you were by the terms of the divorce settlement. I don't understand you. And again, where were you two weeks ago today between the hours of 3:00 and 4:00 p.m.?"

Lucy sensing that Gumby had gained control of the conversation turned sharply to Phyllis and said, "You don't have to answer any questions now!"

But Phyllis brushed her warning aside saying, "No Lucy, I came prepared for that question." She was pulling a receipt from the thin portfolio case she had carried in with her to Dalton's office. "Here you are Sheriff. This is my receipt from a cruise to Cozumel I had started that day with some of the other Sisters of the Needy."

Gumby looked over the receipt and asked, "Who are the Sisters of the Needy?"

Again Lucy jumped in to caution Phyllis, but she only got "Phyllis you don't" out before Phyllis shushed her again., "Lucy it's okay." Then to Gumby she replied, "The Sisters of the Needy are a group of women that pal around together. We're all divorced and on our own. We get together for cruises, spa trips and dinners in Dallas on a regular basis.".

"But that all takes money. You got a bundle when you divorced. So why Sisters of the Needy?"

In a tone of arrogance, Phyllis continued, "Don't you see Sheriff? We're all divorced with nice settlements from ex-spouses. So we can go and do as we please. Kinda like sorority sisters. But some of those exes of ours were left needy by the settlements. So the name fits and a lot of those bastards needed to be left needy. Anyway Sheriff, besides the receipt, I've got more papers to show that I was on the boat at that time that day. Not to mention five other Sisters that I was with who can tell you where I was that day."

Dalton turned back towards Lucy and said," I'm going to want to see all those receipts and have those women in for questioning. I'll need a list of them by this afternoon. Phyllis can cooperate or we can subpoena all of this information. Frankly at this point, I don't care what it is. You two don't ever come charging in here again like that or I'll have a deputy come arrest you for disturbing the peace. If Phyllis wants to cooperate, she can leave the papers with me now along with a list of the women who were with her on the boat. I'll start contacting them this morning. If you have nothing else to say, this meeting is over."

Dalton rose from his chair and opened the door to the outer office. He stood expectantly with his hand on the door knob as Phyllis and Lucy consulted together in whispers still by his desk. In a moment or two they walked over to him. Lucy turned towards Phyllis and said, "Give me everything pertaining to you being on that trip." To Dalton she said, "We'll turn them over, but I need copies of each piece of paper and receipts from you. Phyllis doesn't have anything to lose. While your secretary is making copies and receipts, Phyllis will make you a list of the women and their phone numbers."

"If she has addresses I want those also.", interrupted Dalton.

"Very well Sheriff.", Lucy said frostily. But it will be nice when you quit messing around and try to find the real killer. You know elections are a little over a year away. The citizens of Feaster County might decide they need a real lawman representing them." She handed the papers to Gumby and said, "We'll wait out in Ms. Owens' office while she finishes up. Phyllis will leave the list on her desk. Good morning Sheriff."

As she and Phyllis marched out of his office, Dalton handed the papers over to an obviously nervous Linda. "Take care of these ladies Linda." Then he slammed his door shut and snapped a pencil that he had picked up in two. Back at his desk, he fumed over Lucy Morehouse's "real lawman" comment. But at least if the media called, he could truthfully say he was checking out some new leads even if it turned out to be nothing as Phyllis said it would be. Which is where he thought it was going to end up.

Chapter XIX

Tommy Randall fidgeted in his seat as the teaching assistant droned on through a very dull rendition of "Effective Business Communications" in his computer marketing class. He had filled up on a bacon cheeseburger and double fries in the student union before coming to his 1:00 p.m. Friday class. The mindless babble coming from the T.A.'s mouth nearly put him to sleep. But he would catch himself when he started drifting off and jerk his head back up. Each time he did that, he would glance over at the clock on the wall. Slowly but surely, the time for the class to be over was drawing near. He was staying geared for that moment when he would need to be the first out the door and up the flight of stairs to the next floor where Hootie taught his classes.

Mercifully the TA stopped his droning three minutes early and told the class to have a good weekend. With his long legs, he galloped up the stairs knowing if this was the last class Hootie was teaching today, he would be posting a sign on the door of Tommy's Ag-Marketing class saying that there would be no class meeting today. A reading assignment for the weekend would be posted under the announcement. Tommy learned that Hootie often disappeared right after the 2:00 p.m. ritual. He couldn't be found in his office or anywhere else in Joe Autry Agricultural Building. What he did next was up to Tommy to discover.

One of the coeds was coming down the stairs, her arms loaded with books as Tommy barreled up the stairs. He had his head down focusing on the steps and ran right into her on the landing. Books flew everywhere and she was pushed back against the wall. That kept her from falling. Tommy ended up on his knees.

Highly flustered,his face glowing red with embarrassment to where it nearly matched in color the roots of his red hair. Tommy scampered to his feet and began picking up books. "I am so sorry! I just wasn't watching. Are you okay?"

The coed, a perky redhead herself about five foot-three inches replied, "Well I don't appear to be hurt if that's what you mean. But I've got to get to my next class. This is going to make me late." By then Tommy had picked up the last of her books and put them back in her waiting arms. Tommy looked into her face for the first time since the collision and liked what he saw. She was eying him with bemusement and good humor. Her eyes were twinkling.

He responded, "Me too. I've got to get upstairs to see a professor who I think is going to give my class a walk today. Again I apologize. Maybe I can make it up to you with lunch next week."

"Well maybe so. But I don't even know you."

Tommy's face reddened again to the color of a beet. He broke into a grin that showed off the gap between his two front teeth. "I'm Tommy Randall."

"Well Tommy Randall, I'm Clair McConnaughay." She extended her right hand from under the armload of books.

Tommy took it in his hand and asked, "Clair, how do I find you for lunch?"

"I work in the library every day. Just ask for me there. If I'm out the others there can contact me."

Tommy reluctantly let go of her hand and said, "Okay, I'll call Monday or Tuesday. Now I gotta go." He dashed for the steps, but only to turn around for one last look at Clair. That look caused him to misstep once again. This time he was spread out prone on the steps, his body pointed upwards towards the next floor. Clair was amused, but she appeared to be alarmed as she asked with real concern., "Are you okay?"

Tommy picked up his lanky frame and said, "I think so. Now I really have to go." He headed up the stairs and disappeared through the door onto the next floor. Clair watched him go before resuming her trip down the stairs. She wondered if he would really call her for lunch next week.

Now in the hallway, Tommy hurriedly walked to room 204 where his 3:00 MWF class met. The note from Hootie was already there. It read "No 3:00 p.m. class today. Read chapters 21 and 22 and be prepared to discuss them in Monday's class. Have a good weekend." He groaned at the thought that his collision with Clair might have been just enough of a delay to have cost him his chance to keep Hootie under observation. But he glanced down the hall just in time to see

Hootie lock the door to his office and head for the nearby stairwell. "Dr. McGuire!", he called. Hootie turned and waited for Tommy to catch up with him. "I saw your note on the door, but I thought you told us Monday to have our survey of crop marketing strategies by mom and pop farming operations ready to turn it to you today."

Hootie looked momentarily at a loss, then said, "That's right, I had said that, but I figured you all could bring them in Monday. You're certainly diligent in asking about it."

"Well thanks Dr. McGuire.", blustered Tommy as he got red in the face once again. Hootie entered the stairwell followed by Tommy. In tandem, they walked down to the door that exited to the faculty parking lot. Hootie moved towards his maroon F150 pickup with Tommy trailing behind.

When he opened the truck's door, he looked puzzledly at Tommy, "Do you know where you're going Randall?"

He reddened again and stammered, "Yes sir. My car is parked in the student lot in the next block. I thought it would be easier to get to it coming this way."

Hootie said, "If you say so. See you Monday."

"Okay, see you then." Tommy sprinted to his car parked 100 yards beyond the faculty parking lot and started it up, all the time keeping his eye on Hootie's pickup as it began leaving the lot. He ducked down behind the wheel when Hootie made a right turn out of the lot which drove him right past Tommy headed in the opposite direction than Tommy's car was pointed. When Hootie's vehicle rolled past his car, Tommy sat up fast and, started his car and lurched away from the curb forcing another car coming in the same direction to brake hard to avoid hitting him. The irate motorist honked loudly. Tommy looked into his rear view mirror to see the man following the honking by shooting him the middle finger. But keeping up with Hootie was his main concern and he realized that he was about to lose him again. Racing down to the intersection, he made a quick u-turn forcing an oncoming FedEx truck to brake quickly. Once again his action drew a honking and a middle finger from the braking driver. He got a repeat performance of it from the first driver as he whizzed past him intent on following Hootie.

When he got within a block of Hootie, he relaxed and followed him at a leisurely pace. The drive went about 12 blocks into an area used by Tarleton State to provide housing for its faculty and staff if they needed a place to live in Stephenville. Hootie pulled over to the curb in front of a yellow brick duplex that had separate sitting porches in front of each of its entrances. Sidewalks bordered by a single outside row of yellow and orange asters and a shared flower bed filling the space between them led to each entrance from the curb. A block long sidewalk about 25 feet away from the curb bisected these two sidewalks and others like them up and down the street. Hootie went to the sidewalk on the left and made his way onto the porch. He knocked on the door and stood there awaiting expectantly.

Meantime Tommy had slipped on a baseball cap to hide his red hair as he cruised slowly down the street. He was just at the edge of the duplex when the door Hootie had been knocking opened suddenly. Tommy saw a young woman in her early thirties step out on the porch with a big smile on her face. Enthusiastically she hugged Hootie and planted a kiss on his cheek. She took his arm and led him inside. Tommy had just enough of a look at her to see that she was a very pretty woman, a brunette with the tips of her hair frosted. That brought attention to the flawless skin of her face. Tommy also observed that her curves were just right before she closed the door. He made a quick trip around the block before parking fifty yards or so behind Hootie's pickup. This time he was pointed in the same direction as Hootie.

He settled in to wait for Hootie to reappear. After 15 minutes, Tommy figured out that he might be here awhile and looked around for something to occupy his time. He settled on getting Hootie's reading assignment for Monday out of the way. He opened the book to Chapter 21 and began to read. There was just enough warmth from the sun to make him drowsy. Pretty soon, his eyes closed and his head dropped down on his chest. The book slipped out of his hands and down onto the floorboard. He slumbered lightly dreaming about meeting Clair again in a more conventional setting. Two boys about 10-11 years old came home from school and began tossing a frisbee back and forth to each other. They were out in front of Tommy's car. The boy facing Tommy's car let the frisbee go with more force than before. It sailed over his playmate's head and hit Tommy's windshield.

The plastic dish made just enough noise to waken Tommy. He set up suddenly and saw the frisbee resting on the hood. The two boys were trotting towards his card to retrieve their missile. All of a sudden he noticed that Hootie's pickup was gone. In a panic now, he was assessing what to do next when Hootie's truck came by headed in the direction from which it had come, the Tarleton

State campus. The young woman was seated very close to Hootie. He had a pleased expression on his face as he once again passed Tommy headed in the opposite direction. His eyes glanced over towards Tommy's car as he took in the boys going to retrieve their frisbee. Tommy had ducked down and wasn't seen by Hootie. He counted to ten figuring that was enough time for Hootie to be in the next block. He jumped up starting the engine and turning away from the curb. The boys jumped back as Tommy accelerated, the frisbee still on the hood. His tires peeled rubber as he sped to the next intersection to make another u-turn. Once again another driver was forced to hit the brakes to avoid colliding with Tommy. A professor in the foreign languages department, she not only honked at Tommy and shot him the finger, but let out a torrent of Spanish that left no doubt about her displeasure with his driving. The frisbee had fallen off the hood into the middle of the street halfway down the block. The boys were headed over to pick it up when Tommy ran over it splitting it in two. He never slowed down, but glanced in his rear view mirror to see both boys giving him the bird. As he sped up after Hootie, he reflected philosophically, "At least they couldn't honk at me too."

He glanced at the clock on his dash and discovered it was nearly 6:00 p.m. Hootie had been at the duplex over three hours. What had he been doing?, Tommy wondered. He caught sight of the truck and fell in behind it about two blocks back. Where was Hootie going now? He didn't have long to wait for an answer as Hootie went to Washington Street and drove to the Montana Restaurant, a popular eatery just across the street from the Tarleton campus. He pulled into the customer parking lot and walked around to the passenger side opening the door for the young woman. Hand in hand, they walked into the restaurant. Tommy watched them from the no-parking zone he had pulled into a block back. When they were inside, he parked in another spot on the other side of the customer lot. He entered the Montana Restaurant.

Once inside, he didn't immediately see Hootie and the young woman. There were several dining areas in which they could have been seated. Unsure of what to do next, he decided to go to the men's room and plan his strategy. Besides his bladder was letting him know it hadn't been emptied in over five hours and wasn't going to wait much longer. He stood in front of the urinal relieving himself when he felt a slap on his back and heard a familiar voice. "Hey Randall, I've never you seen you here before.", boomed Hootie who had stepped up to the urinal next to him.

His face beet red once again, Tommy stammered, "Oh hi Dr. McGuire. I stayed over doing some of my studying since I didn't have anything planned for the afternoon and evening. I've been here in the library and realized it was supper time. This is my first time to eat here. Have you been here before Dr. McGuire?"

"Nearly every Friday since last April. I recommend their 12 ounce T-bone. Good thing you got here now. This place fills up on Friday nights. Pretty soon the waiting time will be 90 minutes or more to get a table"

Tommy shook himself and closed his fly. "Well thanks for letting me know. I think I will just get a burger to go at the bar. I need to get back to Honey Oaks. And I want to catch Coach Donaldson on the pregame show as I drive back."

Hootie jumped in, "Tonight is a big game. I rarely ever miss seeing the Bumblebees playing. But you know Randall, I have yet to see to see a Friday game this season. I've only caught that disaster against Turnersborough in Waco on Saturday two weeks ago." Tommy had washed his hands and was drying them under the air dryer on the wall as Hootie made his way to the wash basin.

Taking advantage of Hootie giving him this information, he queried, "Why is it you're missing the Friday games this season?"

"Let's just say I have other interests in Stephenville on Fridays since last April." Hootie was using the paper towels to dry his hands. "And I better get back to my table. She's waiting out there now."

A look of realization came on Tommy's face. "Oh I see. Well I better get to the bar and place my order. See you in class Monday Dr. McGuire."

"See you then Randall."

Tommy wasn't seated long at the bar before the waiter came over to get his order. "Hey Tommy. I've never seen you in here before. What would you like to drink?" It was Charles Crandall who shared two classes with Tommy including the Ag-Eco class taught by Hootie.

"You're right Charles. I've never been here before. But I just saw Hootie in the men's room and he says he's been here nearly every Friday since April."

Crandall answered right back, "Yeah that's right. Ever since he met that TA who's working on her masters. Cindy Golden is her name. For an older woman she's pretty awesome."

"Have you waited on them before?"

"I did some through July when this bar tender job opened for me. I took it because the tips are better. But they rarely ever come in here. They have their special table which the management saves for them. You can count on them to be here before 6:00 each Friday." He winked at Tommy, "From what I gather from talking to Dr. McGuire, they spend every Friday together. He goes to her place over in the faculty and staff residential section right after his 1:00 class lets out. That's why we get so many walks for our 3:00 class. He'd rather be banging her all afternoon than in class talking to us about the economics of crop rotation on the soil."

Tommy's mouth was wide open, "Wow! She seems awfully young for him."

Charles was delighted to share what he knew. "I guess there's something special about him. What it would be, I can't imagine. But I can tell you that after an afternoon at her place, they always get here close to six, have a quiet dinner at their table and then go back to her place for the night. I've heard that Ms. Golden turns her phone off for that time. No one can reach them until the next morning."

Tommy said again, "Wow. Wait til I tell Clayfour."

"Who?", asked Charles.

Tommy remembered he was supposed to be keeping everything under his hat and clammed up. "Oh nothing, I know a friend of his who likes to keep up with Hootie. I just might mention this to him someday. But him knowing Hootie like he does, he probably already knows. Matter of fact, I won't even mention it at all. Oh Charles, I need to get a bacon cheeseburger, both mayo and mustard, but no onions to go. I'll take a big Pepsi in a styrofoam cup also."

He handed Charles $10.00 and waited on the stool for his change. When Charles brought back $4.00. Tommu peeled off two of them and said, "Thanks Charles. I also need a receipt if you'll get me one."

"No problem Tommy, Here you go and thanks. I've got some new customers at the other end of the bar. I better go take care of them. See you Monday." Tommy sipped his Pepsi as he waited for his order. Soon Charles handed him the bag and he headed for the exit. A little bit more oriented to the layout of the Montana Restaurant now, he looked around for Hootie and Cindy. He saw them both seated on the same side of a table in the corner. They each had their salads, but were taking turns feeding each other with the salad forks. The glazed look of love that each of them had in their eyes indicated that the food didn't matter. They could just as well have been sticking their forks in a hay bale and it would have tasted the same as their salads. "Yes siree, Clayfour would hear about this first thing in the morning.", Tommy thought to himself. "He will be pleased with my job."He took one last glance at the couple entranced with each other and headed home to Honey Oaks.

CHAPTER XX

The stands in Mustang Panther Stadium were nearly full on both the home and visitors' sides when Clayfour and Katherine arrived 10 minutes before the kick-off. A cool front had blown in from the Panhandle two hours earlier making the air just right for the game. The couple were both dressed in Bumblebee black pants, the black and gold short sleeved athletic shirts and the special Bumblebee shoes from the Nike Shoe Company. Clayfour carried two light jackets for them that were all black except for the gold and black bumblebees applique on the left breast part of each jacket. They would slip them on an hour or so after the sun set and the night chill began to creep in. They spotted a group of Honey Oaks fans sitting on the 40 yard line who were waving to them that seats had been saved for them. The Petersons made their way down to where they were seated below the concourse. They exchanged greetings with Kim Whittaker, her estranged husband Robert who was there to show their united support for Tad and the rest of the Bumblebee team. Then they greeted Tricia and Wayne Collins—Larry's parents and Felicia Washington and Gene Perkins, the mother and stepfather of Desmond. One row below them were Monica and Paul Robinson, Ryan's parents, To their right were Arnold's parents, Amy and Arnold McCloud, Sr.

As they watched the Bumblebees and their opponents, the Southside Fightin' Bulldogs finish their warmups and retreat to their respective dressing rooms for last minute talks from the coaches, the group jumped around talking about the two things most important to them-tonight's game and Justin's will. Both teams had 3-1 records and were ranked in the top 15 in Class 4A ranks in the state. Honey Oaks was ranked eighth and Southside 12th in the latest Texas High

School Coaches Association polls. This game was also being played up on the sports pages as a showcase for the three Division I prospects that would be on the field tonight. For Honey Oaks, that would be Tad with his impressive quarterbacking credentials. For the Fightin' Bulldogs, it was Marty Tomlinson and Chad Henderson, both senior linebackers, both three year starters, both winning All-State honors last year and both six-feet-five-inches and 275 pounds plus with 4.9 speed. Like Tad, they were hearing from every Division I program possible. None of them seemed to be in any danger of not going to the college of their choice.

In the stands, the Honey Oaks crowd gathered around Kim and Robert to hear them tick off the list of colleges that had jumped on the Tad bandwagon, Texas A&M, Minnesota, Florida State, Notre Dame, Penn State, TCU and virtually every school on the west coast. Not to mention Texas, Oklahoma, Nebraska, Ohio State and LSU who had been sending Tad notes of their admiration and fondness for his skills from his sophomore year on. They all said how well he would fit in and prosper in their respective programs. The other parents could only listen to the impressive list of top universities knowing that their sons might make it with Division II schools or junior colleges or NAIA schools. At least that's where their letters of interest were coming from. Finally Amy McCloud shifted the conversation to another aspect of the world of scholarships, "Isn't it just wonderful that Mr. Slater left the Booster Club all that money for scholarships? That's going to help a bunch of kids over the years."

"Oh yes!", piped in Tricia Collins. "Larry has his heart set on playing for Angelo State. If he can get one of these first scholarships from Justin's bequest, it will make him living in San Angelo that much easier."

The sound of both bands striking up their fight songs drew their attention back to the field. The teams were running out of the big air-filled helmets that were inflated on each team's respective end of the field. The helmets showed off the school mascots and colors on their sides. The fans on both sides of the field were standing and cheering the Bumblebees and Fightin' Bulldogs as they ran to their sidelines. Once they were there, the fans sat back down for the moment, knowing that they would quickly be right up for the school songs and the National Anthem. The conversation about Justin continued. Paul Robinson said, "Everyone here is excited about Justin setting the club up with a perpetual source of scholarship funds, but I heard yesterday there's one person in town not pleased with that."

Amy asked, "Who would that be?"

Paul responded, "Phyllis Slater. The way I heard it was that she wasn't too happy with you Clayfour about it. Did she throw a book at you at the nursing home after you talked to her about the will?"

Before Clayfour could answer, Katherine jumped in and said, "That was true. I was helping a resident in another wing at the time. Word spread pretty quickly and I knew about it almost before Clayfour could get out of the parking lot. But I feel for Phyllis. The pressure of an ugly divorce and then having her children lose their father in such a violent manner must have gotten to her. You know Clayfour and I were the best of friends with them for so many years. I think he was just trying to get her to think about how her actions are influencing what people think about her. She took it the wrong way given the stress she's under." The crowd was getting up as the Honey Oaks High band started to play the school song. So Katherine said no more. But the seed she planted took the pressure off Clayfour and got people to think about the game that was about to start.

Colleyville Southside won the coin toss and elected to defer their choice until the second half. Honey Oaks received the ball, but couldn't go anywhere with it. Tad was calling plays like "Red Right Torch. Split.", but then wasn't getting a chance to execute them. Henderson and Tomlinson the two Fightin' Bulldog linebackers were crashing through the line almost unopposed to either sack him or at least break up the passes. On the other hand, the Bumblebee defense was having the same kind of results in combating the Southside offense. At halftime it was still a scoreless game.

Clayfour got up to go to the concession stand to buy Katherine and him drinks and a bag of popcorn to share. There he ran into two people he had last seen at the Booster Club meeting Monday. The first was Jerry Schilling. The Honey Oaks maintenance man very jovially stood in the line for the concession stand right behind Clayfour. This time Clayfour remembered who he was after Jerry tapped him on the shoulder. "Why hello Jerry. I didn't know you went to all the games, especially out of town."

"As a maintenance man, I've been on call at Barrett Bradwell for each home game. I normally don't do road games, but this one sounded too good to pass up seeing. So when I closed the shop at 5:00, I took off for here."

"So what do you think of the game so far?"

"Pretty ugly. I figured we would be ahead two or three touchdowns by now."

"Yeah those two linebackers are getting to Tad quite a bit. Our line has to give him more protection." Clayfour was now at the head of the line and gave his order to the Southside Band Boosters parents working the concession stand. He paid and scooped up his order nodding goodby to Jerry as he moved past him headed back towards his seat.

Just before he got to the steps leading down to his seats, Tibby Foster came scrambling up. The Booster Club president flashed her always ready smile. "Hi Clayfour. I'm just getting here. All our volleyball games went the maximum number of games. The volleys went on forever. But all three of our teams won their matches."

"Well that's great. Maybe some of their competitiveness can rub off on our football team. You can see that it's pretty tight down there. Neither team can get anything going." Tibby followed him down to where Katherine and the other Bumblebee boosters were waiting. As Clayfour handed a drink and the bag of popcorn to his spouse, Tibby let everyone know the results of the volleyball matches. Everyone cheered the results, then cheered even louder as the Bumblebees made their way back onto the field. After the kickoff which was received by Southside, everyone sat down. Tibby asked everyone in general and no one in particular, "It's been two weeks. Any arrests or suspects yet?"

Clayfour answered for the group, "Nothing yet. I know Sheriff Gumby is checking out a number of possibilities from people with ties to Honey Oaks High and the team to those Justin had dealings with as a broker. His clients, other brokers, etc."

Tibby responded, "Yeah even Phyllis Slater. I heard about the incident at Ingleside Clayfour. My great aunt has a room on that wing. I went to see her Thursday night and she told me what happened that morning between you and Phyllis. She said it could be heard all over the wing."

"Right Tibby, I had been told about her blowing up at the courthouse when Justin's new will was filed. I just tried to tell her that would make her look suspicious to the sheriff. Especially since no one else had been arrested. She didn't take it too well."

Tibby came right back, "If you ask me, Sheriff Gumby ought to focus on people at the school. That's probably where the murderer is."

"Why do you say that Tib?"

"Clayfour, it's only logical. It happened in broad daylight there. Somebody who has the ability to move around the field because he or she is not out of place there, but is an accepted presence is who the sheriff ought to be focused on. If an outsider showed up, he or she might have stuck out like a sore thumb. So Gumby should spend more time investigating the Honey Oaks crowd."

"Including your Booster Club workers?"

"Including the Booster Club workers. Of course this is my hunch and I know nothing about solving crime."

Her comments hit home to Clayfour, but it seemed like Coach Donaldson was the only one who could have had an opportunity. Gumby had indicated he had a valid alibi for going to the Bee Hive which had checked out. His attention was drawn back to the field where the game had moved into the fourth quarter still a scoreless tie. Honey Oaks had the ball. The Bumblebees had moved from their 15 to the Fightin' Bulldog seven with five minutes left to play. Tad had the team back in a quick huddle to hear him call the first down and second down plays. He called," Red Right Z Angle". That would send his wide receiver on the right, Desmond into the middle after Tommy Fordham, the wingback on the right had run to the right sideline drawing two defenders with him. It left Washington free in the middle to take Tad's pass five yards deep and step into the end zone. If he was stopped at the one or two yard line, Tad had called, "Red-Left Tight-Halfback Slam" for the second down play. With all five linemen blocking at a slant, Tad would hand off to Scott McCormick, the senior running back who lined up to his right. He would run through the two hole for the score.

But just behind the defensive line of Southside, Marty Tomlinson and Chad Henderson had different results planned for Tad. When Ryan Robinson snapped the ball back to Tad, Marty had faked right, then came straight across the middle. His big right hand shoved Ryan aside as if he was a matchstick. Chad just bowled over Arnold McCloud from his outside linebacker position. He feinted left, then went inside over Arnold's right guard position. The two big Div-I prospects got to Tad at the same time. Before he could get a pass off or hit the ground, Marty had stripped the ball out of Tad's hand. Chad picked it up on the bounce and took off for the other end zone. Collins caught him from behind at the Bumblebee 18. Only 3:50 remained in the game. The Fightin' Bulldogs were in field goal range at the worst. Tad was mad about the breakdown of his protection. He called the offensive line together as they went off the field. "Hey guys, you've got to give me time. Keep those goons off me. We can do this when we get the ball back. If you want to have Tarbaby down in the briar patch tomorrow, just hold those blocks long enough for me to find a receiver."

Colleyville had moved to the Honey Oaks 10 and faced third and two. Washington, lined up at cornerback,gave the Bumblebees the break they needed. He blitzed and caught Joe Lincoln, the Bulldog quarterback handing off to Trent O'Hair, the back lined up behind him. He smashed violently into both of them and sent the ball flying. Ryan from his left end defensive spot beat the crowd to the ball. He hit the ground cradling the ball in his arms just as a whole crowd of Bumblebees and Fightin' Bulldogs fell in on top of him. The referees cleared the pileup and signaled Honey Oaks' ball when they had peeled off enough players to get to Ryan and the ball he protected so well. Honey Oaks was on its 16 with 2:10 left in the game. The goal was 84 yards away.

Tad was cool as he strapped on his helmet and led the Bumblebees' offensive unit out on the field. He called, "Red Right Torch. Split", but overthrew a wide-open Desmond. With receivers split left and right on second down, Tad dialed his own number with "Double Tight A Seam". He took the snap from Ryan and watched his receivers go down three yards and make 90 degree cuts both right and left. The defensive coverage followed them leaving a gap in the line. He was through the five hole between left guard and left tackle. Those two linemen had pancaked the defenders in front of them. Tad was all the way to the Bumblebee 48 before the Southside safety caught him.

On first down again, the linebacking duo of Tomlinson and Henderson showed that they still had to be dealt with. They blitzed Tad and sacked him for a 10 yard loss. The clock had ticked down to 1:38. Tad's pass on "Red Right Z Angle" worked only for five yards before Desmond was tackled. Facing third and 15 at his 43, Tad called "Trips Right, Y-27 Wheel". Collins went down five yards on the right and curled back to pull in Tad's perfectly thrown pass. As the Southside safety bore down on him, he faked a spin right, then came back around to his left and got 23 yards down to the Southside 34.

With no timeouts left and the clock down to 50 seconds, Tad decided to cross up the defense and called "Red-Left Tight-Halfback Slam" again. It caught Southside by surprise and McCormick got eight yards on the play. But the clock continued to run and only 28 seconds remained when Tad spiked the ball to get time to talk to his team. He hurriedly pulled them together as the referees set the ball. "Okay guys, we're going to dance with the girl we brung to the dance. We will go 'Red Right Z Angle' on third down. Desmond you're the man. If we miss, then on fourth down, it's back to you Larry. 'Trips Right Y-27 Wheel' again.

We're going home in regulation time." Desmond caught the ball over the middle and got six yards before Tomlinson smashed into him. The play took 15 seconds before the refs stopped the clock to move the down marker for the first down. Then the ref signaled the clock to start. The fans on both sides of the stadium were on their feet and yelling for their team to score or to hold 'em. The noise was so deafening that Ryan couldn't hear Tad's signal calling. Confused he snapped the ball as Tad was looking the other way. It bounced off his hands and dribbled left. Tad ran after it and picked it up on the bounce. Instead of staying in the pocket for his throw, he was running for his life going left away from the zone where he was supposed to hit Larry with his toss.

Meantime Larry ran his pattern and saw Tad's dilemma. Seven years of playing pass and catch with Tad at Murphy Park gave him the instinct to give Tad a different target and route, one that they had practiced many many times. He waved at Tad and broke left toward the end zone. When he was at the 10, Tad stopped and planted his feet for the heave towards Larry. Henderson slammed him to the turf right after he released his throw. The next thing Tad was aware of was the horn sounding to end the game. He raised up on his elbow and saw Larry gather in the throw as he crossed into the end zone. The Honey Oaks side of the field exploded in celebration. The hometown Colleyville Southside side was bathed in stunned silence.

The Bumblebee boosters were all jumping up and down hugging each other. Clayfour hugged Katherine, then Larry's mother, his father and Tibby. Then he looked out on the field to watch the spectacle out there. The cheerleaders and the Honeybees had run out and joined the team in celebrating the win. He saw Tara Ann, Dana, Sharon and the rest of the Honeybees giving each player a hug and a high five. The Honeybees didn't stop their celebration with just the players. Each of the six coaches on the field also got a hug and an enthusiastic hand shake. Clayfour watched the celebration until Donaldson called the team to come together on the 10 yard line. When they grouped together there, Clayfour took Katherine by the hand and headed for the parking lot. Even with the dramatic win, it would be a long late drive back to Honey Oaks. And Tommy was due in his office no later than 9:00 the next morning for the report on Hootie.

CHAPTER XXI

Zero Tolerance

It took a long time to get back to Honey Oaks. The visitors went down on the Mustang Panther Stadium field to celebrate with their Bumblebee team. It looked like everyone from Honey Oaks had poured out on the field in celebration. Clayfour saw others copying the Honeybees and cheerleaders in hugging and patting anyone associated with the team, players, coaches trainers and Mr. Rasco. Jerry Schilling was embracing both Tad and Larry at the same time. The mothers of the players stood back from the team beaming and proudly waiting for their sons to come out of the scrum and give them a hug. That was a signal to the moms that it was okay for each of them to plant a kiss on her son's cheek. The dads stood by grinning and waiting for their wives to be done so that they could embrace their sons in a bear hug. The coaches were the next receipients of the accolades from the adoring fans. After a half hour or so, the fans began to go to their cars and trucks for the trip home. Some needed to get gas or drinks or make a pit stop before the stores began to shut down for the night.

About 3000 fans came from Honey Oaks. The traffic going home was long and slow-moving. It was 1:30 a.m. when Clayfour and Katherine got to their home. They immediately fell into bed and were fast asleep quickly. The barking of a dog down the street woke Clayfour up. He glanced over at the clock and saw it was 8:40. He jumped out of bed and into the shower. He dried off and threw on his clothes. In the kitchen, he chugged down a gulp of orange juice straight from the container, took a banana out of the fruit bowl and a bottle of water out of the refrigerator. Then he ran out to his truck parked in the circular driveway in front of his house, started it up and took off for Peterson Gin.

Tommy Randall was out in the gin yard moving equipment to a covered shed. The clouds were gathering and growing darker, a promise of rain perhaps later in the morning. Clayfour was 10 minutes late getting there. Tommy gave him an exuberant, "Good morning Mr. Pete, er Clayfour!" as he climbed out of his pickup.

"Morning, Tommy. Sorry I'm late. We didn't get back from Colleyville til 1:30 this morning. I overslept."

"Yeah, I listened on the radio. What a win! Wish I could have been there to see Tad hit that pass to Larry."

"Oh, it was a game you don't soon forget. But how did it go in Stephenville? Come in to the office and fill me in."

Tommy followed Clayfour in. They were seated together at the small round table which was used by Clayfour for informal discussions with his visitors. He offered Tommy a water or a can of soda from his compact office refrigerator. He popped up and brought him back a Pepsi. Then he sat down and listened intently as Tommy gave almost a minute by minute description of his encounters following Hootie. He left out the details about his mishaps and near mishaps. He rightly figured that Clayfour wouldn't be interested in his collision with Clair and the near wrecks he caused trying to keep up with Hootie. Tommy noticed how much Clayfour's interest peaked as he told about Hootie's love interest, Cindy. Then Clayfour's intensity waned as Tommy told him of Hootie's talk with him about not making any Honey Oaks games which in turn was confirmed by what Charles Crandall told about Hootie's and Cindy's regular dinner dates at the Montana Restaurant.

Clayfour asked Tommy a few more questions and thanked him for his efforts. Then he said, "Did you keep receipts on what you spent to do this for me?"

Tommy said, "Oh yeah, here you are." He pulled a wad of three different receipts out of his jeans pocket and offered them to Clayfour.

Clayfour said, "I'll have Diana cut you a check for these and your time on Monday. Would you say you had eight hours in it?"

Tommy scrunched up his forehead and began to calculate, "Well, let's see. I started at 2:00 when class was over. It was nearly 7:00 when I left the restaurant. It took me an hour to get home. I guess it was more like six hours Clayfour."

"That's okay Tommy, I'll pay you for eight. You certainly earned it."

"Wow! Mr. Pete, er Clayfour, Thanks a lot. Let me know if I can do this again." He waved as he left the office.

Clayfour watched Tommy drive off. Then the other phone on his desk rang abruptly. "Peterson Bail Bonds".

"Mr Peterson please.", came the female voice over the line.

"I'm Clayfour. You've got me."

"Yes sir, this is Deputy Williams. I'm the jailer here at the Feaster County Detention Center. We've had a DWI locked up overnight that's now sober enough to release on bail. He wants you to bail him out."

"Well, just go ahead and do it as we normally do. Isn't it the usual $5,000.00?"

"Yes it is, but there's a special request from him for you."

"Who is it and what does he want?"

"It's Jerry Schilling. Apparently he went to the game in Colleyville last night and celebrated the Honey Oaks win too enthusiastically. He bought two six packs on his way out of Colleyville. By the time he crossed into Feaster County, he had downed eight cans."

"Besides bailing him out, what does he want from me?"

"A ride home.", replied Deputy Williams. "He missed a curve about eight miles from here and totaled his vehicle."

That concerned Clayfour enough to ask, "Did he get hurt?"

"Not really, a few cuts and bruises. You know how some drunks get lucky when they're three sheets to the wind and just bounce like a rubber ball unharmed when they hit? That's Mr. Schilling. As I said, he totaled his pickup and asked if you would give him a ride home."

Clayfour glanced at the clock and saw he would have enough time to get Jerry home before he had to meet Dalton at Danny's. "That'll be no problem. I'll be there in 30 minutes. Get the bail papers ready and bring him out please when I get there."

"No problem Mr. Peterson. He will be ready".

"Thank you."

Thirty minutes later Clayfour was in the Detention Center signing bail papers. He had stopped at the Honey Oaks Gas N' Go to buy Jerry a big cup of coffee and a tin of aspirins before going to the jail. As soon as he had finished his paperwork, he sat by the entrance to the drunk holding tank. Jerry emerged very red-eyed and wobbly on his feet, but sober enough to be released. He spotted Clayfour and started towards him. But the movement staggered him. Clayfour jumped forward and gave him support. "Here Jerry, take this coffee and sip it. Let's get in my truck." The two shuffled out to the pickup slowly, but surely.

Once he was in the passenger seat and belted in, Jerry threw his head back and sat there with his eyes closed, a pained expression on his face. Clayfour took two aspirins from the tin and opened Jerry's left palm to deposit them. "Here Jerry take these and some more coffee."

Jerry complied, then said his first words since coming out of the cell. "Clayfour I really appreciate your coming. I sure messed up. I should have known better."

"What do you mean Jerry?"

"Just simply, I have a drinking problem. I can't tolerate any alcohol at all. But I got so excited with our win last night I just decided to celebrate. What a mistake! My drinking is what split me and my wife up 10 years ago."

"Have you always been a heavy drinker Jerry?"

"No. It used to be just a couple of beers on a hot night or on the weekend. But then when I got fired from my job at the metal plant so unfairly, I began to drink all the time."

"Why did you get fired unfairly?"

Jerry began his story with a lot of sadness coming on his face as he detailed what had happened to him on the job. "After my discharge from the Army, we were living in Illinois. I took a job with a local metal fabricating company that turned out all kinds of finished steel products. After I had been there a while, I began to hear about people in the next town down river from the company getting very ill, mostly cancer-like symptons. Some of them were even dying after a year or so with their symptons. I finally realized that the company was discharging its slag waste into a holding pond that actually was right by a stream that fed into the river. During the rainy times of the year, the holding pond would overflow right into the stream. Those people were becoming ill and dying because the company I worked for wasn't tending to controlling the hazardous waste coming out of the holding pond right into the water supply for that town."

"So how did that cause you to become a heavy drinker?"

"Well Clayfour, I couldn't stand to see no one doing anything about that problem. It was like management could have cared less. They didn't want to spend the money for fear it would cut into their bonuses. So I decided to inform the governmental authorities about it. Thought I might even get a reward for calling attention to a problem that was sickening and killing a lot of people."

"So you became a whistleblower in effect, huh?"

"I guess that you could say that. But it was a big mistake. For my efforts, I got nothing in reward money. Worse yet Clayfour, the company fired me on the spot after they got investigated. They figured out it was me who turned them in. There was no recourse for their actions against me. And getting another job around there beacame impossible to do."

"Is that when you started your drinking?"

"Yes, I started hitting the bottle real regularly, from the first hour of the morning until late in the evening when I would fall asleep in a drunken stupor."

"I guess this was when the troubles started with your wife. Probably it got to be too much for her to handle?"

"That's right Clayfour. She tried to be understanding at first, but I was just so devastated that I did nothing to help the situation."

"Jerry I guess that since she was the only one working that the bills started stacking up on you.?"

"Yes, she finally threw up her hands and said she was done with me and the situation that I had gotten us into. So she filed for divorce and moved out. I didn't fight it. I did join AA and gained some control over my drinking after that. I even got a job as a maintenance man at a car dealership up there. It allowed me to barely get by. Then Mom got sick for the final time and I moved back here to take care of her. That was what I told you the first time I saw you at the stadium. By the way, do you mind if I smoke?"

Though Clayfour hated having the smell of stale smoke that would be left when he let Jerry off at his house, he agreed to it "just once" knowing he wasn't too far from Jerry's house. Jerry lit up, drew on his cigarette and exhaled a puff of smoke. "Thanks, smoking is another vice I can't get rid of. I average a pack a day."

"Do you mean you smoke on the job?"

"Oh no Clayfour, not at all. The Honey Oaks ISD has a zero tolerance policy about smoking. If I got caught, they would fire me in an instance."

"So you never even try it?"

"There is one place where I can smoke and never get caught."

"Where is that?"

"Out at the stadium. There's an indentation in the stadium wall that I can get behind and not be seen. I have to be out there on game days and do it regularly. No one can see me at all when I'm there. But I can see everyone coming and going inside the stadium."

Clayfour pounced on the obvious question. "Were you in that spot the day Justin was murdered?"

Jerry paused, took another drag on the cigarette and answered reluctantly, "Yes I was."

"When?"

"Shortly after 3:00 that afternoon."

"Did you see anyone go to the Bee Hive?"

"Justin of course followed by Coach Donaldson in a few minutes. Then Coach Donaldson came out and went to his office."

"And that was it?"

"No there was another person after that."Jerry went on and told Clayfour about the last visitor to enter and leave the Bee Hive.

"Jerry That's huge! You have to know how the sheriff has had no luck in solving this in two weeks. Why didn't you come forward with this?"

"I told you Clayfour. Zero tolerance. I was afraid I would get fired if anyone knew I had been smoking at the stadium Besides I just told you how I lost my job and my marriage and became an alcoholic from trying to come forward when people were getting sick and dying.It did nothing for me then. So I had vowed never to be in that position again."

"But Jerry, this is different. Justin was our friend from way back. I am glad you told me what went on. At least we now have a lead that may bring an end to this hunt for Justin's killer. I'll bet the school district will overlook your smoking if Justin's murderer is caught."

"You're right Clayfour. I guess I need to talk to Sheriff Gumby. I have been avoiding him when he's been out to the school the last two weeks trying to question people for any leads. I would see his car coming and make myself scarce and hope that he wouldn't get around to asking me if I knew anything."

"Yeah he's been real frustrated in getting anything concrete out at Honey Oaks High to help him solve this. Because I had spent 10 years away from here in police work before I came home to take over the business after Dad's stroke and subsequent death, I have been helping out by talking to people who had business connections to Justin. Sheriff Gumby would have gotten to you at some time

Jerry. If it's okay with you I can tell him what you have said this morning to me. He and I are going to have lunch together at Danny's right after noon."

"That will be fine. I need to go to bed for a while before I face the world."

"Good Jerry, I'll be discreet and just talk to him. I bet your job won't be in any trouble for coming forward. This will get checked out by him." They were parked in front of Jerry's house by now. He opened the door, nodded goodby and slowly walked to his front door, a big burden removed from his shoulders by talking to Clayfour about what he had seen.

CHAPTER XXII

Zero Tolerance

Clayfour had 15 minutes to get to Danny's when he let Jerry off. He accelerated his pickup to 15 miles over the speed limit to try to beat Dalton to the eatery. He wanted to get his order in for a smoked turkey sandwich before the sheriff got the two of them the rib platter again. But Gumby was already there and had placed the order. Pam was bringing their sweet teas as Clayfour walked over to the table out on the patio. It wasn't the same table that they had used before that had given them some privacy to talk. This table was in the middle of a group of five or six other tables. It meant that they would have to talk softly or not at all.

"I thought I told you I was just going to get a sandwich this time."

Dalton chuckled, "Hey it's on me and I always take the leftovers home. So just don't eat too much."

"Well thanks buddy, you don't have the weight problem I do. But one of these days it'll catch up with you."

"I'll switch to smoked turkey sandwiches when it happens. So what did you uncover in Colleyville last night and with your college boy this morning? By the way that sounded like a heck of a game."

"Yes it was. Tad and Larry clicked for us. But Desmond's fumble recovery and our line's blocking on that final drive sure helped us get the win. I didn't really learn that much from watching the game except for one observation. Let me tell you about Hootie and Tommy first."

Pam came up with the big tray of steaming ribs then. She set it in the middle of the table. Then she produced plates, a knife to cut the two racks of ribs into individual servings and a bowl of wet cloth towels to supplement the roll of paper towels on the table. The big tip from Dalton last time had been remembered by Pam. She had the cook put three extra ribs atop the two racks in expectation of maybe an even bigger tip this time. The two each took a couple of ribs and put them on their plates. Dalton grabbed the squirt bottle of sweet sauce and squeezed more on the ribs even though they were already dripping in the sauce.

Clayfour chewed slowly and talked softly of Tommy's account of following Hootie. The look on Dalton's face grew gloomier as he learned of Cindy and a witness that could verify Hootie being in Stephenville on that Friday and nearly all other Fridays since last April. "It's just like I predicted on Thursday. We've lost both Phyllis and Hootie as prime suspects."

"What happened to Phyllis?"

Dalton told Clayfour about the brouhaha at his office Friday morning with Phyllis and Lucy Morehouse. "I took her paperwork and talked to three of the five women that she said were on a cruise in Mexico with her two weeks ago. They verify her story and said they would come forward if they need to. One of them even has a group picture of the Sisters of the Needy taken at a port in Cozumel. Phyllis is in it and it's dated the day Justin was killed."

"The who?", queried Clayfour, his face showing clear puzzlement.

"The Sisters of the Needy. It's a group of divorced rich women who get together to party. They claim they left their ex-husbands needy in the divorce settlements they got. Thus that name."

"Ooh, pretty cold group I'd say.", reflected Clayfour. Then he brightened and said, "But I had Tibby Foster, the new Booster Club president tell me at the game that she thought it had to be someone tied to Honey Oaks High and the football team or booster club who could move around the stadium without drawing any attention because he or she was supposed to be there. Then just about an hour ago, I got the word of someone fitting that description who was seen going into the Bee Hive after Coach Donaldson had come and gone."

Dalton threw a rib back excitedly on his plate and asked, "Who was it? How did you find out?" Dalton's raised voice in asking the two questions had diners at the other tables looking their way. Clayfour noted this and responded in a very low voice which couldn't be heard at the nearby tables. He told about bailing out Schilling, giving him a ride home and learning how Schilling's avoidance of the

zero tolerance policy against smoking had allowed him to see a person that neither one of them had thought of as a suspect. He named the person and said that
he was available to go check him out as soon as they got through eating. Dalton
responded that he needed an extra 15 minutes before he could meet up with
Clayfour at the suspect's residence.

Clayfour said, "I know where he is living. He's rented that little house back of
Delbert Dulaney's place on Travis Street. I'll head over there and start checking
everything out. Just get me some backup soon."

Dalton replied, "You need to be careful. You might want to wait on us."

"I've got my Glock locked in my glove box. It's going into my shoulder hol-
ster under my jacket as soon as I get out to my truck. I'll be okay. That's a pretty
good equalizer."

Clayfour arrived at the Travis Street residence a few minutes later. He was
parked across the street from the main house so that he could look down the
driveway at the little house in the back. A car in the driveway had Honey Oaks
High faculty parking stickers on it, a sign of someone being in the little rental
unit. Just as he was about to open his door, a car came from the other direction
and drove into the driveway parking just behind the car in the back. This one also
had Honey Oaks High stickers on it, but for student parking. In a moment Tara
Ann got out of the car and walked to the door of the little house. She was clad in
a black and gold Bumblebee sweat suit. At the door she didn't knock, but pushed
it open and went on in. She was unaware of Clayfour watching her across the
street.

For a couple of minutes, he considered this unexpected development and
decided to go ahead as he had planned to go to the rent house. But his curiosity
was aroused. How did Tara Ann fit into the picture? Why was she here? He
treaded softly down the driveway to the house. Opening the screen door, he tried
knocking on the solid core door. Tara Ann had apparently not shut it tightly after
she got inside because Clayfour's knock pushed it open again. He saw Tara Ann
standing across the room, her Honeybee sweat shirt laying on a chair beside her.
She was braless and before she could cover herself with her arms, Clayfour saw
her beautiful breasts that were well-developed, more than any other 16 year old
girl he could ever remember. Just behind her stood the Bumblebee line coach,
Derrick Lindholm. He was clad only in his briefs from which his erection bulged.

Clayfour took in the scene a little longer while the couple looked back at him in wonderment as to why he was there. Finally it clicked in his mind again what his initial thought on seeing Tara Ann undressed had been. A 16 year old girl tremendously developed, but still just 16. Lindholm was a year out of Texas Tech and at least 21 or 22. Clayfour exploded, "Tara Ann's under age Lindholm! What do you think you're doing?" Lindholm reacted with rage as his strong arms on his six feet-six inch, 260-pound body reached out and pulled Tara Ann back against him. Tara Ann screamed while she continued to try and shield her breasts from Clayfour's view. Derrick had one arm around her neck and one around her waist.

He yelled back at Clayfour, "Why are you even here? You're invading my house and getting into my private activities which don't even concern you!"

"Coach Lindholm just for the record, I was a Dallas cop for 10 years and know what constitutes statutory rape. And I've known Tara Ann all her life. She definitely is too young for you to have sex with." At this pronouncement, Tara Ann began to wail steadily. She was embarrassed but scared to be in this predicament.

Clayfour answered Lindholm's question, "I'm here because you were seen going into and leaving the Bee Hive the day Justin Slater was murdered. A witness says you were the last one seen there before Justin's body was found."

Tara Ann struggled to turn around and face Derrick. "Is that true Derrick? Why would you have even been there? What's going on?"

Lindholm's cool was completely gone now. He bellowed, "I went to the Bee Hive because Slater had called me to come see him. When I got there, he told me he knew what we were doing Tara Ann. He said he was going to turn me in to the Honey Oaks Police Department. When he said that I snapped and attacked him. I hit him a couple of times and knocked him off balance. Then I grabbed the Stinger Sticker and stuck it in him. He went down immediately on his back and I drove it into his body as deeply as I could. Then I got out of there and kept preparing for the game."

Tara Ann was hysterical, "Derrick this is awful! I had no idea!"

"But baby I loved you and didn't want it ruined. And it doesn't have to be. I can take care of Peterson right now and no one will ever know. You'll see!"

With that pronouncement, Lindholm tightened his grip around her neck and waist and began inching closer to Clayfour. He moved very quickly and shoved Tara Ann aside as he leaped for Clayfour. She hit the floor, her breasts uncovered as she put out her hands to brace for the fall. All the time this had been going on,

Clayfour had kept his hand inside his jacket on his Glock. When Lindholm jumped toward him with outstretched hands reaching for his throat, he had just enough time to pull the Glock out and fire one round at Derrick's feet. He had kept his shooting skills up to date. His intention was to only disable Lindholm from making the attack and keep him from doing any other harm. Derrick screamed as Clayfour's bullet found its target in his left ankle. He went down immediately grimacing in pain.

By then, Dalton and two of his deputies had arrived. They called for an ambulance to come treat Lindholm before taking him on to the hospital and to check Tara Ann for possible injuries. But she was still more embarrassed than hurt and scrambled to get her sweat top back on. Clayfour related what Lindholm had said that clearly identified him as Justin's killer. The soon to be ex line coach sat there in handcuffs and listened as the trauma crew attended to his wound. When they had fixed it up enough to continue on to the hospital, they rolled him out on a stretcher accompanied by a deputy guarding him. Stunned he looked back at Clayfour and asked, "How did you ever find me?"

"It was a violation of the zero tolerance policy that got you."

"Zero tolerance for murder?"

"No, smoking."

The bewildered Lindholm protested as the stretcher reached the door, "But I don't smoke!"

"You're right, but Jerry Schilling does." Lindholm's face was one of complete puzzlement as he was wheeled out the door to the ambulance.

Epilogue

A Saturday in October, Two Years Later

It was deafening in the Cotton Bowl as the Texas and Oklahoma football teams faced each other in their annual clash. The fans of both teams were roaring their loudest in a din that virtually drowned out any attempts by the Longhorn and Sooner quarterbacks to call out the plays to their respective teams where they could be heard. Instead they were relying on hand signals to get the word out what the next play was going to be. Tad sat on the Texas bench, his uniform unsoiled as he was the backup quarterback for the Horns. He had yet to get in the game which was late in the fourth quarter. The Sooners led the Horns 10-7, but Texas was driving with the ball when the starting quarterback was leveled by a Sooner tackle penetrating the Texas line. Though he held on to the ball, he appeared to be unconscious on the field. Mack Brown told Tad to warm up as the Horns' trainers raced out on the field to tend to their fallen player. It was evident after it took them several minutes to get him on his feet that Tad was going in. There were 90 seconds left in the game when Tad called three plays in a row in the huddle. Quiet still prevailed in the Cotton Bowl as the fans on both sides were watching to see if a stretcher would have to be called out to take the quarterback off the field. But he finally got to his feet and left the field with two of the trainers holding him up. The crowd applauded for him.

It was second and 17 when Tad took over on the Horns' 48. He wasted no time in giving the Horns the lead. He found his wide receiver 10 yards behind the Oklahoma safety at the Sooner 20 and put the pass right into his hands. As the receiver scored, Tad was mobbed by his teammates. They were pounding on him and jostling him in celebration. Tad woke up as the jostling continued. It was his roommate Larry Collins trying to waken him. They were on the Angelo State team that was playing West Texas A&M at two o'clock. Larry said, "Tad you're having your Cotton Bowl dream again yelling out plays in your sleep. You've got to quit so I can get some sleep!" Tad stared dazedly at Larry and then over at the alarm clock on his bedside table. It was 3:15 a.m. He had been having this dream continuously since arriving at Angelo State in early August to play for the Rams.

He ended up going to Angelo State because of a severe injury that he had suffered in the first quarter of the second round playoff game for Honey Oaks two years earlier. Early in that game, Tad was hit high and low when he went back to pass. The high hit, a helmet into his chest, bent him straight back. The low hit came from the side landing squarely on the outside of his right knee. The ripping and tearing sound that accompanied that hit was a signal to Tad and everyone else there that his playing days as a Bumblebee were over. He might not even have a college career to look forward to. When Tad was gone, the Bumblebees folded and exited the playoffs earlier than anyone in Honey Oaks thought would happen.

The ACL injury was so severe that virtually every college that had been courting him dropped off the radar screen. It didn't help that in addition to the ACL injury, he had his paroneal nerve severely damaged. That limited his ability to flex his right ankle. Scholarship offers disappeared as fast as they had first been extended. It took him over a year of rehabilitation ands several surgeries for Tad to get back whole again. But that didn't bring all the Div-I schools back knocking on his door. He was damaged goods. Only Angelo State stood ready to give him a scholarship to play for the Rams.

*   *   *   *

Back in Honey Oaks at the same time as Tad was awakened by Larry, Clair Randall was awakened by the sound of a crying baby or perhaps two of them.

Sleepily she rolled over in the bed and shook Tommy awake. "Honey it's your turn. Teresa or Teddy is awake. Go see if it's a diaper or a bottle that's needed."

Tommy groaned and sat up on the edge of the bed. Seeing the 3:15 hour, he groaned again and said, "Clair, I'd swear that I was the last one up with them at midnight."

"That's right Tommy, but I had to take care of Teddy two hours ago. I didn't waken you when I went to their room. Now go see who's crying and why." Clair briefly smiled at Tommy, closed her eyes and rolled back over. Tommy sleepily went to the twins' nursery, a bedroom down the hall which they had to reconfigure when Dr. Latham detected two heartbeats when he examined Clair in the sixth week of her pregnancy.

Tommy stumbled into the room that was lit only by two night lights plugged into wall outlets opposite each other. The crying was coming from the baby bed adorned in blue colors including the bumper pad. "It must be Teddy.", he reasoned. Still Teddy and Teresa were so identical in looks with the flaming red hair that came from both their parents that Tommy only knew for sure who he was attending to when he checked their diapers to see if one needed to be changed. This time he was right about it being Teddy. He changed his diaper, gave him a bottle as he held him tenderly while he rocked in the big rocking chair that was placed opposite the two baby beds. The bottle and the repetitive motion of the chair soon put Teddy back fast asleep. Tommy put him back in his crib and went back to his and Clair's room. As he climbed back into bed, Clair snuggled up to him as if to show her appreciation and love for him as her husband and the father of the first two of the seven children they would ultimately have together.

*   *   *   *

In Bateman Hall at Tyler Junior College, Tara Ann gazed at the clock and its 3:15 a.m. reading on that Saturday. She was excited about being a member of the Apache Belles dance team. Later that day her group would be the halftime performance in the game between the Apaches and the Navarro Bulldogs. It would be her first time to dance as a college student. After the arrest of Derrick Lindholm, she had been the center of attention and inquiries about how she came to be involved with him. In short order, everyone in Honey Oaks knew about her being called Tarbaby and why. Leslie had been shaken by what had happened to her daughter and the notoriety it had heaped on her and the family. She delved deeper into what had happened to bring Tara Ann into the promiscuous behavior and low self-esteem that she finally realized had characterized her daughter the last few years. It was more than normal teenage sexual awakening involved here. After getting Tara Ann into counseling and sitting down and talking with her, it came out that a former brother-in-law of Leslie married to her older sister, Jeri, had been sexually abusing her from age four on up. Tara Ann had been told by him that she and her whole family could get badly hurt if she told what was going on. It had to remain their secret according to Uncle John. The pattern of abuse went on unchecked for several years before the marriage of John and Jeri ended in divorce. It became so a part of Tara Ann's lifestyle that she thought that was the way she had to relate to all other males. Thus the descent into the sexual practices that had set her up for the notoriety that came with her being called Tarbaby.

She received counseling all through her senior year and also dealt with being a witness in both the trials of Derrick and her former Uncle John. When she had disclosed what he had done, Leslie and her dad had filed a criminal complaint against John and got him arrested and charged for inappropriate sexual behavior with a minor. But she got through all those traumas and began to feel good about herself again just before her graduation with the help of the counseling. She realized that she didn't have to act in a promiscuous manner to be attractive to the boys at Honey Oaks and the college guys who began to show interest in her. She continued to be active sexually, but now limited herself to someone she was in a steady relationship with. Her dancing skills had been noted by Tyler and it offered her a scholarship to come be a part of the Apache Belles. The scholarship was accepted and she threw herself into being the best dancer and student that the school could have. She was able to put the abuse behind her and move into a new way of life. The name Tarbaby remained behind in Honey Oaks in the tales that were told by the boys who would never forget their times with her for years to come.

*   *   *   *

His growing prostate caused Leon Rasco to wake up to make his hourly trip to the bathroom at 3:15 a.m. in his retirement cabin at Red River, New Mexico. He had moved to the mountain resort town in January nearly two years ago when he went ahead and asked the school board to let him take early retirement. The board had graciously consented to his request after seeing how much the stress of dealing with the arrest of Lindholm and the subsequent unveiling of the details about Tara Ann had unnnerved him. Once word was out how she got to be called Tarbaby and why and how it related back to the ninth grade English class where Uncle Remus was introduced to the class, many parents and would-be reformers called his office to protest that being part of the curriculum for those students at such an impressionable age. Enough calls came in that he was directed by the board to inform Patty Barnes that she could no longer have the works of Joel Chandler Harris included in the studies of southern American writers. Instead despite her protests, she was told to add John Grisham's writings to the class assignments and teachings. To further make sure that all mention of Tarbaby disappeared from school materials, the librarian, Glenda Lightsey was ordered to destroy copies of Harris's books that had been on the shelves of Honey Oaks High. She too did so under great protest. Both those women were less than civil towards Rasco even though he was just the messenger in this case following the orders of the school board. The board in turn had listened to the text book committee after all the negative publicity had flowed in over the whole incident. The murder of Justin Slater had pushed him to the edge of wanting to get out of the education business. Catching his murderer and the upheaval that followed put him over the edge. Save for his prostate, high blood pressure and other assorted ailments that came with his age, Red River had been a great place for him to be far away from the stresses of school life. Patty Barnes chose not to continue at Honey Oaks High. She moved on to a Louisiana school system that was more appreciative of her plan of teaching when her contract was up at the end of the school year. Lightsey had only one more year to reach her magic number of 80, years of education service added to her age to equal that number. When it was done, she was done. She took retirement after the next year and traveled with friends to all the places that she had only known about through the books on the library shelves.

*   *   *   *

Clayfour liked his work in helping Dalton solve Justin's murder enough that he volunteered to help on future cases if Gumby needed him. The sheriff immediately took him up on his offer and utilized his investigative skills to find out who had killed Dick Nichols. It turned out to be one of his property management clients who felt that Nichols was overcharging him for services or not even providing them in some cases. He was able to pull away from the everyday management duties at Peterson Gin and Peterson Bail Bonds some since his son Harold Clayton Peterson V or Hal as he liked to be called had graduated from Texas A & M the year following Justin's murder.He came home to take over some of the duties with the family businesses. Clayfour became known as the man to go to for the hard crimes and relished in resuming his police career in a private investigator role. At 3:15 a.m. he and Katherine were now asleep in the Hilton at College Station. Later that day, they would watch their beloved Aggies take on conference rival Texas Tech at Kyle Field before driving home after the game.

*   *   *   *

As Derrick's trial approached, Dalton had to deal with Kim in gathering information for the trial. The district attorney used him to get details about anyone involved in the murder. With Kim having discovered Justin's body along with Leslie, she became someone that Dalton saw a lot to gather evidence. Soon a mutual attraction developed between the two lonely singles. They found themselves seeking comfort in each other's arms. It was not unusual for Kim's neighbors to note that Dalton's cruiser was many times parked all night long at her house. They thought that she was getting really good protection as a star witness in the upcoming trial. But when the trial ended with Derrick receiving a 50 year sentence and the cruiser continued to be there at night, they concluded that Dalton and Kim were an item after all. And right now, they were asleep for another two hours before they would rise at 5:15 a.m. to get ready for the trip to San Angelo to see Tad, Larry and their Ram teammates play West Texas A&M in the 2:00 conference game.

978-0-595-42386-6
0-595-42386-8

Printed in the United States
81481LV00002B/811-924

9 780595 423866